V891i

THE
INHERITANCE

Also by Claudia Von Canon
The Moonclock

THE INHERITANCE

Claudia Von Canon

Houghton Mifflin Company Boston 1983

Library of Congress Cataloging in Publication Data

Von Canon, Claudia.
   The inheritance.

   Summary: When Miguel de Roxas, a young nobleman
studying medicine in Padua, is summoned home to Spain
to claim his inheritance, he is plunged into the
tumultuous events resulting from the treachery of the
Inquisition.
   [1. Inquisition—Spain—Fiction].   I. Title.
PZ7.V889In   1983   [Fic]   82-23418
ISBN 0-395-33891-3

To the memory of my father

THE INHERITANCE

ART 1

he auto-da-fé had to be delayed by half an hour. It was to be held at four o'clock in the afternoon of St. John's Day in the Year of the Lord 1580 at Madrid's Plaza Mayor, a spacious rectangle bordered on three sides by brick houses. On the wrought-iron balconies the ladies of the nobility were already sitting, protected by awnings from the blazing sky. The grandees, in black with white, ruffled collars, filled the tribune, making a somber contrast to the gold-embroidered vestments of the clergy, the white cowls of the Dominicans, and the crimson robe of the Cardinal Great Inquisitor. A cordon of soldiers, each wearing a breastplate that blindingly reflected the sun, was holding back the populace. The mood of the crowd was festive and eager.

Bundles of wood had been stacked in the center of the square. There were also ten gallows, hastily erected. Sixty men in flame-colored gowns and wearing pointed dunce caps were now brought forth, but only fifty of them were to be burned. Ten of the condemned, singled out by royal mercy, were to be hanged before the official beginning of the ceremony.

Yet King Philip counted only nine. The Master of the Holy Office had to confess to him that one of the men had managed to swallow poison in the dungeon, unaware of

3

the favor His Majesty had bestowed on him. It took the monarch a while to ponder the case and to choose one from the fifty unfortunates to replace the dead man so that the last gallows would not be idle.

Then the Act of Faith began, without further ado. While the stakes were burning and the screams of the victims mingled with the clergy's chants and the people's responsories, King Philip thought of the prisoner who, by duping the hangman, had now certainly gone to eternal damnation: Juan de Roxas, former royal physician, until recently in retirement at Saragossa.

Toledo's charterhouse contained twenty-four cells, each one opening into the flower-filled inner quadrangle of the cloister. In twenty-three of them, their cowled tenants were reciting Compline, the evening prayer. A soft murmur filled the courtyard, punctuated from time to time by the calls of the swallows darting in and out under the arcades.

From the twenty-fourth cell no sound was heard but the scratching of a quill on paper. Presently it ceased.

"That will do, Vega. Now call for lights." The voice was even, almost casual.

"At once, Your Eminence." The secretary rose and withdrew.

Don Pedro de Talavera, Cardinal Great Inquisitor of Spain, spurned the Palace of the Holy Office, with its swarms of clerics, scribes, soldiers, petitioners, and confidence men. He had installed himself in a cell at the charterhouse, where he would be undisturbed. He was accustomed to working at night, by the light of many banks of candles. His known dislike of the dark had the Toledans whispering that he was afraid the souls of the many he had

4

sent to the stake or to the gallows would crowd his dreams. No one knew whether those ghosts haunted him. Had anyone dared to ask him about his practice, he would have answered that he lightened his nights to lengthen his days, which he knew to be numbered. Many years ago, before the walls of Saint Quentin, he had received a bullet between his ribs. Although he had almost forgotten about it, it was still lodged in his body. Every day it moved infinitesimally closer to his heart.

Vega returned with the monastery's candle keeper, who knelt and kissed the cardinal's hand, then lit a half-dozen tapers in silver holders. He had also brought a candle in a pewter stick mounted on a little mirror to double the light of its small flame.

As the cardinal closed his eyes and leaned back in his chair, his spare frame disappeared under the folds of his crimson robe. Vega looked at his master, trying to surprise that face, fine-boned, hollow-cheeked, implacable, in an unguarded moment. So far he had not succeeded.

The cardinal opened his eyes. "The reports."

There were several messages from abroad, among them one from London. He read it with a frown. Why must Elizabeth be such a splendid ruler, shrewd, thrifty, cautious, yet seeing every advantage and pressing it? Don Pedro respected the heretic Queen out of a spiritual kinship and thus was all the more distressed by the behavior of her opponent Mary Stuart who, though in prison, squandered Spanish men and Spanish money on a lost cause. He would have to see to all that.

He moved the foreign dispatches aside. It was his rule to take care of domestic matters first. There was this business of the Jews at Saragossa. They had been brought to trial on the charge of having stabbed a Christian child to use its blood in their secret rites. Their guilt seemed clear. They had been convicted and condemned to the stake. But what about Juan de Roxas?

He had been brought in as the Crown's expert and, after examining the child's body, had given only a guarded opinion. According to Gil de Vega's report — the secretary had been present at the trial — the court, noting the doctor's reluctance to make a clear statement, had ordered a search of his house. In the cellar there was found evidence that he had given shelter to a number of Jews, some of whom had fled in the meantime. When these charges were brought forth, Roxas had turned witness for the accused.

"My life is forfeit," he had said. "I may as well speak the truth. That boy was never killed in the Jews' house. He was choked beforehand and brought there afterward. There was little blood on the body, proof that he had been stabbed after death to make it appear a murder by knife."

Reminded by the judge that he was implying that Christians had killed a Christian child, a crime so monstrous as not to be believed, the doctor nonetheless had insisted on his statement. Since he refused to recant, he was condemned along with the others. The next day they found him in his cell, poisoned. He had drunk the liquid in the tiny glass vial he had been wearing on a thin chain around his neck.

"Any family?" Don Pedro asked.

"A son, Your Eminence, by the name of Miguel. He studies at Padua. Roxas himself had been widowed for several years."

"What about his estate?"

"The house in Saragossa has been searched and sealed."

"Any subversive books or writings?"

Vega consulted the protocol.

"No, Your Eminence. Mostly works on medicine, physics, and botany. The *Iliad* and the *Odyssey*, Aldine edition of 1500. The *Confessions* of Saint Augustine. Cicero, Seneca, Tacitus, Catullus. And two dozen letters from Monsieur de Montaigne."

"Let them be sent here."

"Your Eminence?"

"Yes?"

"The protocol says they have been burned."

"Burned? Why, may I ask?"

"Your Eminence, Padre Domingo has declared Monsieur de Montaigne *persona non grata* with the Church of the kingdom after reading those letters."

"I see." The cardinal's voice betrayed none of the slight irritation he felt at this excess of zeal on the part of Padre Domingo, the Inquisition's commissioner at Saragossa.

"Your Eminence . . ."

Don Pedro merely raised his eyebrows. Vega's words died on his lips, but he brought himself to speak with the courage of greed: "Will the Holy Office take possession of Roxas' house?"

"No."

Vegas' mouth almost fell open, but he pressed his lips together in time. Don Pedro looked at his secretary with a weariness akin to disgust. Privy to the inner workings of the Holy Office, he thought, you have not learned anything. You do not yet know that one does not make enemies needlessly. Roxas had to die, for he had failed to acknowledge that the Church's truths pre-empt all other truths. But to take his possessions, to give the house to you,

7

Gil de Vega from Saragossa, who obviously covets it, would be a mistake.

What did the Florentine have to say on that subject?

If the Prince has to shed blood he should be careful not to touch the victim's estate, for men will be quicker to forget the death of a father than the loss of an inheritance.

If I take Roxas' possessions, the son will never come back. He will be full of hatred and anger. Quite possibly he will join the rebels in Flanders. If, on the contrary, I leave the estate untouched, the young man will enter his inheritance gratefully. He may even think that his father acted rashly, by not awaiting royal mercy. He will, in due time, become a faithful servant of the King, who has not many of them.

Those thoughts were not uttered. Don Pedro disdained to impart them to his secretary. He merely said: "Write to Miguel de Roxas. Bid him to come home."

n a summer morning the weekly mail barge from Venice slowly made its way up the Brenta Canal toward Padua. Two boatmen steered her, gondolier-fashion, each with a long oar. It was market day. At each stop peasants, carrying baskets full of eggs, vegetables, and fruit, as well as live chickens in crates, would board the boat amid chatter, laughter, and noise, unmindful of the more distinguished city folk who had come aboard at Venice for the short trip to the university town.

By noon the domes and towers of Padua appeared against the blue sky, and soon the barge pulled up at the customs house, where a sizable crowd was waiting on the landing: townspeople, clerics, beggars, and students in their black garb, a long foil in the belt, sporting sometimes exaggeratedly pointed hats. Many of them came from other Italian cities or from abroad. They would meet the mail boat every week in the hope of news or, better still, a letter of credit from home.

Master Zani, the letter carrier, hoisted a canvas bag over his shoulder and made his way up the steps. He preferred delivering his mail then and there, rather than dragging it all over town, so he would pull the letters out of his bag and call out the names on the envelopes. Whenever there was no answer he would, as often as not, throw the letter away.

He sat down on a stone bench, the young men crowding around him like so many blackbirds in hope of a crumb. He opened his bag and fished out the first missive. "Giovanni Spina!"

A skinny youth held out his hand. His face registered disappointment as he received the thin piece of paper. "No money in it. Nothing but good advice. I can just feel it."

"Vitus Tracterius! That's the fourth letter within six weeks! What a faithful girl!"

Vitus Trachter, a broad-shouldered Tyrolean, blushed up to the roots of his red hair. Father Radurner, the village priest, who had been instrumental in sending the bright boy to Padua, wrote frequently, giving him news of family and neighbors, births and deaths, seeds and crops, and never omitted to mention kisses from Cilli, his penitent and Vitus' patient sweetheart. Yes, she is faithful, Vitus would have liked to say, but seeing the mocking eyes of his companions, he merely snatched the letter from Zani and sat down to read it.

"Maurizio Baiardo!" Zani italianized the name of a portly young Frenchman, Maurice Bayard. "No respite from those cutthroats, eh?"

It was the third reminder from the House of Mocenigo in Venice that the student must repay a loan of fifty scudi with the interest. Zani knew the worries and joys of his customers. After several other communications he drew out of the bag a thick, official-looking parchment. "Miguel de Roxas!"

There was no answer.

"Say," said Vitus, who had read his mail and joined the

circle again, "I could bring it to him. What a thick hood! They probably made him a count palatine!"

Zani shook his head. "Can't. Royal seal. To be hand-delivered."

"Miguel — Miguel, wake up!"

Gently the girl tugged at the strand of dark hair that fell over the eyes of the young man beside her. She knew them to be deep blue; the color never ceased to surprise her. If he would only open them! But he merely reached for her with a sleepy, yet peremptory gesture.

"Angiolina, you are no bonus for an anatomist. Your ribs are too hard to find. What time is it?"

"Noon. The Saint is ringing. Don't you hear?"

Indeed, the cathedral's bells were in full swing. After a long while they came to rest, their last ring trembling away in the sunny air, leaving behind a plaintive death knell, which sounded from a little campanile nearby.

"Whom are they burying?" Miguel asked.

"It's Monna Aldruda. I forgot to tell you."

"Is that right? The bats must be rejoicing."

Aldruda was an elderly widow whose frenzied fear of bats had made her something of a butt to the townspeople and a source of income to generations of street urchins, since she would have them catch and kill the creatures at the rate of three quattrini a dozen.

"Don't laugh, Miguel. Bats will drink your blood at night." The young scientist gave her a look that was half pity and half scorn. "Have you ever seen one sucking away at someone's throat?"

"No, not I, but . . ."

"Then don't talk rubbish. Bats couldn't draw blood if

they wanted to. They're blind, to begin with; couldn't even find you. Aldruda, *requiescat*" — Angiolina crossed herself — "was a fool. I wonder whether Acqua got her brain."

Girolamo Fabrici d'Acquapendente, professor of anatomy at the university, eagerly dissected heads of madmen and madwomen whenever they were available.

"I should think so. She left no family."

"Good. I'd like to take a look at it. It's probably all twisted." He pulled his arm from under her neck. I'll get up in half an hour, he was about to say, when he heard Monna Gianna, the landlady, making her way up to his room, the old wooden steps groaning under her weight.

She knocked.

"Signor Miguel! What a slugabed! There's a letter for you."

"Push it under the door, please."

"Can't," came Zani's voice. "Too thick. Besides, I need a receipt."

Miguel jumped up, threw on a few clothes, flung the coverlet over the giggling girl on the bed, and opened the door for the mail carrier. In return for his hastily scratched signature he received the bulky envelope.

"A pleasant afternoon to you, Signor Miguel," Zani wished him, and, richer by three soldi, tramped down the stairs.

The letter owed its thickness mainly to the heavy second hood and the ponderous seal. Its contents were brief.

In ten lines it informed Miguel de Roxas that his father, Dr. Juan de Roxas, erstwhile physician to His Late Majesty, Emperor Charles V, and afterward to His Majesty King

Philip II, had died by his own hand while being detained in protective custody by the Holy Office, thus forfeiting the possibility of royal clemency. His son and only heir, Miguel de Roxas, was invited to return to Spain to take possession of his late father's estate. If the said son, Miguel de Roxas, did not present himself at Saragossa within the next three months, the estate of the late Dr. Juan de Roxas would fall to the Crown.

The letter was signed and sealed by Gil de Vega, secretary to His Eminence Don Pedro de Talavera, Great Inquisitor to the Kingdom of Spain.

The lines burned themselves into Miguel's brain, yet he felt no pain. Recently he had seen a thief's right hand cut off. As it lay bleeding and still twitching on the executioner's block, the man had regarded the severed limb with a silent, weary curiosity. Now Miguel could comprehend that benumbed state. He knew, as well, that the apathy would not last.

"Angiolina," he said in an even voice that sounded oddly loud to his ears, "get up and get dressed. Run to the Bursa and find Vitus. Ask him to come here."

She rose at once, with the tact of loose women who have learned to read a man's face and thus, unlike their chaste sisters, know when to refrain from questions.

The door closed behind her.

Cautiously, almost stiffly, Miguel sat down on the bed. Something told him that as long as he did not stir, the monster that lay in wait for him would sleep.

Within half an hour, Vitus arrived. Miguel had not moved. The letter still lay on the table. The Tyrolean gave his friend a worried, questioning glance, answered by an imperceptible nod. He read, and a fear settled over him in the sunlit room, as if — so the saying went in his mountains — someone had walked over his grave. It lasted no longer than the batting of an eyelid and left him more angry than shaken. This was not the time for senseless fancies, he scolded himself, but for standing by his stricken friend.

He folded the letter and put it back on the table. Then he said, "What will you do?"

"I must go home."

"Miguel, you are out of your mind. This is a trap."

"Most likely."

"Then why don't you stay here? You ought to be glad to be out of their clutches."

"And let those bastards take the house and sit in my father's chair . . . ?"

The dam broke. A burning tide of pain washed over him, making him gasp for breath. He understood with every nerve of his body that he would never again see his father, never again look into the thoughtful eyes, never again enter the quiet study for a reassuring talk, with a bottle of Rioja shared between them.

No. He would not — could not — allow himself to dwell on that, not so long as terrible questions remained unanswered.

Protective custody? Someone must have denounced Juan de Roxas to the Holy Office. But who? And why?

Dry-eyed, his head aching, Miguel began to think aloud. "My father lived alone, Vitus. He had only a small circle of friends. Of course he disliked the King, disliked him intensely. But who would ever tell on him? The Montoyas? Never. Paca? No. Or could she have talked out of turn? How? Father hardly discussed his political views with her . . ." He ran on, making assumptions, rejecting them, his thoughts racing in circles.

Vitus listened quietly, without reminding Miguel that he was talking to him mostly in riddles, speaking of people whom he, Vitus, did not know.

By nightfall, when Miguel had reached a state of feverish exhaustion, Vitus went down to the market square to fetch some food and a bottle of wine. Passing by an apothecary shop, he went in and bought a vial of valerian. Back at Miguel's quarters, he spread the victuals on the table: bread, cold chicken, fennel salad, and oranges.

Miguel tried to eat, but the food stuck in his throat. He reached for the wine, which Vitus had laced with the sleeping draft. Hardly had he emptied his goblet when he leaned over the table, buried his head in his arms, and sank into forgetfulness.

Vitus picked him up and laid him on the bed. Then he cleared away the dishes, took a chair, and began his vigil.

Miguel suddenly began to stir uneasily, his brows furrowed, as if he were tormented by nightmares.

Vitus regarded the sleeping figure with unaccustomed detachment. So it has happened, he thought. A blow has fallen on that privileged life. He thought back to the day he had first met Miguel in a crowded lecture hall, more than a year ago. Professor Acquapendente had been expounding on the function of the liver, talking rapidly in his colloquial Latin while displaying a chunk of brownish, spongy stuff in a glass. Vitus had been utterly lost until his bewildered glance was caught by the young Spaniard, sitting next to him, who had quickly sketched and labeled the organ in the Tyrolean's open notebook.

After the session Vitus had thanked his colleague. Miguel,

pleased and also a little curious about the quiet mountaineer who stood apart from the other, more boisterous students, had invited Vitus to lunch at the Ox, Padua's foremost tavern. Over risotto and a bottle of Valpolicella, they got to know each other, laughing, perhaps to cover their discomfort, at the grotesque disparity of their backgrounds.

"Still, we will both be quacks," Miguel had remarked, "authorized to prescribe syrups."

"Yes, but I wonder how long it will take me," Vitus had replied, with a worried frown.

He was having no easy time at Padua. His academic preparation was sketchy at best. He had learned what he could from the village priest, who had taught him whenever the family could spare the boy from work — which was not too often. Thus put at a disadvantage, he frequently had to study far into the night to keep abreast of the lectures. Moreover, his sponsors, though enthusiastic, were poor. He had to supplement his income by clerking for the law professors and to content himself with the cheapest quarters in town, the Bursa, a house for needy students. He was eager to win his diploma, to secure a position, and to show his gratitude to all the good men and women who had put their trust in him.

Miguel, on the other hand, in easy circumstances, was in no hurry to leave the university. Of keen, passionately inquisitive mind, he took to his studies naturally, while at the same time he reveled in the more sensual pleasures that life in Padua offered.

Soon after their first encounter, he had announced to Vitus that he would tutor him in Greek and anatomy. Though Vitus was at first puzzled by the offer and uneasy about the many hours Miguel proposed to spend over the books with him, he soon understood that these sessions provided his colleague with a certain sense of domination, as well as with the opportunity to clarify his own concepts by imparting them to another bright mind.

Miguel had also insisted on teaching Vitus to fence, appalled by the farmer's lack of a skill necessary day and night in a town full of brawling students and prowling ruffians. Disregarding his friend's good-humored protests, he had dragged him to the fencing ground and had begun to put him through the paces of swordsmanship with a perplexing singleness of purpose. Concern for Vitus' safety alone could not account for the tyranny with which Miguel conducted those lessons.

The young Spaniard fenced splendidly, well served by his slim, supple body. Vitus, though as tall as Miguel, was heavier and slower. The swift thrusts of swordplay were alien to his limbs, used to ploughing and woodchopping.

Yet Miguel seemed to be spurred on rather than discouraged by this lack of natural talent in his pupil. He wanted to see, with an intense, detached curiosity, how far he could coax quicker reflexes from his friend's strong but reluctant muscles.

Vitus, streaming with sweat, would not always appreciate the experiment, but he would give in again and again before the radiant satisfaction in Miguel's eyes whenever a perfect attack-riposte-attack would crown the efforts of a strenuous hour.

Those evenings of instruction, however, though frequent, were bound to no schedule. Whenever Miguel wished to spend time with Angiolina or one of her several substitutes, or preferred to go for a stroll, join his colleagues at the Ox, or take the barge to Venice, the lessons were canceled, often with little or no notice. Vitus did not resent it, for the most part. He had grown grudgingly fond of Miguel and was content to enjoy the young Spaniard's exhilarating company whenever it was available. Still, under his friend's wit and grace, Vitus soon detected an arrogance which, at times, he found hard to stomach. Whenever he was reproached for his high-handed ways, Miguel would answer with a laughing impenitence that both pained Vitus and disarmed him.

There had been the incident with Cecco. He was Monna Gianna's grandson, a quiet, dark-eyed youth, slightly misshapen. Cecco had courted a girl in the neighborhood. Coyly, she had encouraged him, until the day a more welcome suitor appeared, when she had shown Cecco the door. The following night the boy had cut his wrists.

Miguel, returning late from the Ox, had invited Vitus to come up and have a last bottle. After some drinking and chatting, the Tyrolean took his leave, and Miguel was lighting him down the narrow staircase when they noticed two rivulets of dark liquid oozing from under Cecco's door. It was locked from the inside. Within seconds, the two young men had broken into the room.

In the light of a candle guttering in its tallow, they could see Cecco lying on the bed, deathly white, but still breathing. Miguel snatched the pillow from under the boy's head and had Vitus press it against the two cut veins. Then he took his dagger, ripped the sheet to shreds, and speedily bound up both wounds. He made two tourniquets, but the blood still flowed, soaking the linen strips.

"Quick! Cola's shop!"

Vitus understood at once. Clay was needed to help coagulation. Because the apothecary had closed for the night, he had to get it from Nicola, a sculptor living next door. He ran down, pulled the indignant artist out of bed, had him fill a bag with clay, and was back almost before he was gone. They wet the clay, made a paste of it, and applied it to Cecco's wrists.

For twenty-four hours they watched him, loosening or tightening the tourniquets, checking the clay, and making their patient drink raw chicken blood. But as soon as the youth was out of danger and feebly asked his rescuers why they had not let him die, Miguel, declaring that he had no intention of listening to Cecco's dreary tale of woe, had left him to Vitus' gentle care. Half-jokingly, Vitus had remarked that such impatience with the simple-minded, the slow-witted, was downright ungodly, since "of such was the Kingdom of Heaven."

"Right," Miguel had replied, "so they have no business boring us down here." And Vitus, in spite of himself, had laughed.

The night wore on, its passing hours struck by Padua's many church bells. Vitus watched Miguel toss and turn, and wondered apprehensively about his friend's decision to obey the summons from the Holy Office. He sighed. With his usual common sense he thought of the errands that had to be run before Miguel could leave. Accounts had to be settled with Monna Gianna; a place had to be found to store books and belongings; he also would have to see about a horse.

He got up, busied himself among Miguel's clothes, and began to pack a coat bag for his friend.

* * *

ollowing the path of the sinking sun, the *Doncella* cut through the waves. She did not need to rely on the wind, sixty-oar galley that she was.

Miguel de Roxas stood on the ship's bow, where the salty breeze was free of the stench wafting up from the rowing benches. He had never traveled on a galleon before; he had always been on sailing ships. Had it indeed been two weeks since the morning he had received the cardinal's letter? The past days, to him, seemed no more than one long hour.

The faithful and levelheaded Vitus had taken care of matters, had procured a mount for Miguel, and had even persuaded Monna Gianna not to rent the young Spaniard's quarters for at least two months. Thus, Miguel had been able to leave the next evening for Genoa.

After arriving at the town's Upper Gate, he had looked down at the Ligurian seaport, spreading in a semicircle on the slopes of a steep hill, its houses, churches, and palaces descending like the rows of a giant amphitheater toward the ship-filled harbor, with its forest of masts, sails shortened and pennants flying. From his vantage point, Miguel had easily spotted the streamers of a Spanish galleon.

Jostled by soldiers and sailors, his ears ringing with cries, songs, and curses, Miguel had a hard time approaching the ship, but luck was on his side. The Duke of San Millán, Admiral of the Royal Armada, had just boarded the galleon bound for Barcelona. Answering Miguel's hastily penned petition, he had allowed the son of his former physician to join his party aboard the *Doncella*.

A gentle finger touching his shoulder recalled Miguel from his musings. It was one of the duke's attendants. "His Grace desires to talk to you, sir."

Over planks and ladders, through the covered passage under the ship's heaving oars, Miguel followed his guide astern to the duke's quarters.

Rodrigo Sanchez de Vilas, Duke of San Millán, had been named Fleet Admiral by Charles V. His devotion to the late Emperor had been boundless. He often said that his own life ended the day Charles closed his eyes at Yuste.

Sitting in an easy chair, his back propped up by an extra pillow, he received Miguel and waved his attendants away.

"What was it with your father, Roxas?" he asked, not acknowledging the young man's bow.

Under its tan, Miguel's face drained of all color. The duke seemed not to notice.

"News travels fast, you know, and suppressed news travels twice as fast. You might have honored me by telling me the whole truth." Without waiting for Miguel's embarrassed answer, he went on: "Your father was a man of honor, Miguel de Roxas. Many more such as he will be caught in the wheels of this hellish machine. And when it has destroyed them all, it will have broken the kingdom. I thank God that I shall soon leave this earth to join my Emperor. What ails the King? The Jews would like nothing better than to be his loyal subjects. And they know how to handle money . . . The new Christians? They are the only ones who work . . . Look at this ship. Built by them, every plank and beam. We are cutting off our own hands..."

The voice lost itself in an inaudible murmur. In the silence that followed, Miguel could hear the rhythmic splash of thirty pairs of oars and the no less rhythmic panting of three hundred pairs of lungs. But suddenly he felt that the ship was floating on the spot. The oars were resting.

"God's thunder!" the duke exclaimed. "They are not pulling up the canvas?"

He touched a bell. "Get me the captain," he ordered the entering attendant, "and hurry."

Miguel, about to withdraw, was checked by a gesture from the admiral.

The captain appeared and explained to the scornful duke that, for all he knew, a case of demonic possession was manifesting itself on one of the oarsmen.

"He is as stiff as a board, Your Grace, and just cramped to his gear. He got a few whacks, but it did no good."

"Ship's surgeon is drunk, I presume."

"Yes, Your Grace," the captain admitted.

"Roxas," said the duke, "you had better go down and take a look. Show him the way, Captain. Don Miguel de Roxas has studied medicine at Padua; that is more than your quack can boast of any day."

Through several short passages inside the ship's hull Miguel followed the captain until they arrived at a heavy oaken door leading into the center aisle of the oar deck. It opened. Miguel reeled back. The smell of sweat and excrement, ever present on the ship but mitigated by the sea wind, assailed him here as if a foul rag, hot and wet, had suddenly been slapped over his nose and mouth. The long, vaulted deck was already plunged in semidarkness, except for a few torches held in rings along the wall. In their flickering light Miguel beheld the creatures who rowed the ship.

Chained five deep to the rowing benches, filthy and half-naked, they hung, moaning, on their resting oars. But there were also curses, prayers, raging quarrels. Some of them were singing in high, crazed voices.

A child of his century and a medical student to boot, Miguel was not squeamish. On Gallows Hill, where he and his colleagues went for dissection material, he had witnessed executions by the dozen. Yet never had he seen men dehumanized and reduced to draft animals, as they were here. It enraged him.

The ship's provost, whip in hand, came down the aisle. "It's the number one on the fifth bench, Captain."

The prisoner in question was sitting stock-still, his hands clenched around his oar, staring straight ahead. He must have been a handsome figure of a man long ago, with his finely chiseled features and slender limbs. Miguel could not take his eyes off him. There was something about the man's rigid position . . . His brain, searching for what he knew was hidden in the recesses of his memory, finally brought it up. The lecture on the Sweet Sickness! Incurable, Acquapendente had said, but easy on the physician, since it saved him the trouble of an autopsy. In a victim of that disease, rigor mortis would set in within a quarter of an hour.

"Untie him," Miguel said. "He is dead."

"Impossible, señor. Look."

With the stick of his whip, the provost indicated a fresh welt on the man's back.

23

"I struck him half an hour ago, and he was quite alive then. He could not be that stiff. No. He must be possessed. I have sometimes seen them like this." He crossed himself.

"Nonsense. It's the Sweet Sickness."

"The what?"

"The Sweet Sickness. It stiffens them almost imme ——"

Miguel bit his tongue. What would be gained from convincing this brute that the man was dead? That no demons dwelled in the miserable hull? He would merely throw the corpse into the sea and have those wretches here resume their torture, but an exorcism might take time and allow them some rest. Science could go hang. "You may be right, after all," he said. "But this would concern the ship's chaplain. Let me call him."

He made for the door and, once outside, drew the deepest breath of his life. Now for the priest, he thought with savage satisfaction. Christ descended into Purgatory. Let this servant of His Church go down to Hell for a while.

As the chaplain, visibly reluctant, climbed down into the hold, Miguel regained his stand at the bow. The *Doncella* was rocking gently on the waves. After a short while two sailors brought a strange form out from the hold. It looked like a wooden sculpture of a sitting, emaciated man, arms stretched out in front of him. The two men pitched it into the sea. Immediately afterward the *Doncella* shot forward, pulled again by thirty pairs of oars.

He thought the crossing would never end. The *Doncella* kept close to the coast, avoiding encounters with prowling Moorish pirates, thus lengthening the journey by several days. Yet little by little the outline of the mountains to the starboard was changing; the small, whitewashed towns dominated by squat, ocher-colored harbor fortresses kept slowly gliding by; Marseille's lights shimmered one night; and finally the *Doncella* let down anchor in the port of Barcelona.

The duke, who was returning to his ancestral home at Burgos, had offered Miguel a place in his traveling party, since he was passing by Saragossa, but the young man had declined with thanks. Making the journey with the duke would have meant at least one idle week at Barcelona, because the old man intended to rest before letting his bones be rattled by Spain's wretched roads.

Although his money was dwindling, Miguel bought a horse. He was pressed for time. It had taken the cardinal's letter four weeks to reach Padua, and Miguel by now had been on his way almost a month. For all he knew, the cardinal might be counting the delay from the date of the letter and be making ready to seize the estate. There was not a day to lose.

From Barcelona he set out on the old Roman road leading west over the Meseta, the high plateau with its reddish earth covered by heather under a hard, clear sky. Villages — or, rather, clumps of three or four brick hovels around a small church and a well — were few and far between. Sometimes a peasant, riding a donkey or driving a bunch of ragged sheep before him, would greet the traveler with grave courtesy: "Go with God, señor."

When he heard it first, after so many months, Miguel felt the sting of tears. This was his homeland. But was he coming home?

Once or twice he put up for the night in a village priest's house, where he was offered a soup of chickpeas, and the horse was allowed to graze in the cemetery. The next day, at the cry of the curate's scrawny rooster, he would be up and back in the saddle.

At last he descended into the Ebro Valley. There, in the clear distance, he saw Saragossa's Leaning Tower, all red brick, emerging from red brick roofs and flanked by the dome of the red brick cathedral.

His heart beat faster — why? There was no one waiting for him. A few more hours and he was crossing the stone bridge, whose seven pillars stood like rocks against the racing Ebro. Once within the walls, he took the "straight lane," which led to a small square bordered by four town houses, each of brick with eaves of cedarwood under the roof.

A tall, slender woman, dressed in black silk, crossed the lane. She was past her first youth, but she moved with the proud grace of the Aragonese. Followed by a maid, she was walking to Vespers. Suddenly she saw horse and rider, hurried forward, and clutched at the reins. "Miguel!"

He jumped from his mount and threw his arms around the lady. "Soledad de Montoya! Doña Solita!"

"Praised be Jesus and His Holy Mother that I caught you! Miguel — you must not go near your house."

"And why not?"

"Come with me. I will show you why."

They walked a few steps, Miguel leading his horse by the reins. Suddenly Doña Soledad stood still and looked with distress at her companion. "Miguel," she whispered, "you do not know . . ."

He took her arm and steadied her. "Yes, Doña Solita," he said gently, "I know."

They walked again in silence.

On entering the house — the square's stateliest — Doña

Soledad motioned a servant to stable Miguel's horse. Then she stepped into the patio, followed by the young man.

"Why, Miguel, what the devil . . ." Don Fernando de Montoya rose from his chair, his handsome old eagle face expressing surprise, pleasure, and concern. A glance from his wife told him that Miguel apparently knew of his father's death.

He embraced the young man and looked him over. "Padua is doing you good," he declared. "Why the hell did you come back?"

"He must not go to his house," Doña Soledad pleaded.

"She is right, Miguel. We had better show you."

Doña Soledad led the way to the balcony looking out on the square. The Roxas house was basking in the last evening rays, which gave its bricks a warm glow and were reflected by a band of green and blue tiles running under the grilled windows. The great entrance door was locked. Attached to its right panel was the seal of the Holy Office. Two soldiers stood guard before it.

Miguel turned to his friends. "I expected that much," he said, "but they summoned me."

He produced the cardinal's letter.

" '. . . died by his own hand . . .' Praised be God!"

All the time he was on his journey, Miguel had both wished and feared to learn how his father had died. Don Fernando did not wait for him to ask the dreaded question. He put his hand on the young man's shoulder.

"Miguel," he said, "a bitter draft should be drained at once. You know the worst already. But as to how it came about, I will tell you. A child's body was found in a Jew's house, stabbed through the heart. Since the synagogue was burned, the Jews were accused of holding their rites in that place and of having murdered the boy for their idolatry, as it is called. Padre Domingo, our new town inquisitor, who likes to be called the Just One, asked for an expert opinion. The next day your father was personally summoned by Gil de Vega, the cardinal's secretary, who happened to be in town . . . Let me see, has he not signed your letter?" Don Fernando again unfolded the paper he was holding and quickly glanced at the signature. "Vega, as I said, called him into court to examine the body. That was the last we saw of your father. None of the townspeople heard him testify, because the trial was held secretly — God knows why they needed an expert then — and the Jews were found guilty and packed off to Madrid, your father with them. It took us more than a week to find out that the court proceedings had long been over and that those wretched Jews already on their way to the bonfires while we were still waiting for the outcome and for your father to return. I hurried to see the padre. Losing no time over the question of guilt or innocence — they can make anybody guilty whom they want guilty — I pleaded with him to ask for royal clemency in the case of your father.

" 'Clemency has been granted,' he told me. 'The gallows instead of the stake.'

"I asked whether the sentence had been carried out, but he kept silent. This letter, at last, tells us that your father has found his peace."

Motionless, Miguel listened to Don Fernando's tale. If it brought no comfort, it at least offered some explanation of events.

"Your mother was spared this," Doña Soledad said softly. "God took her in time."

Silence filled the flowered patio.

Don Fernando was the first to speak again. "Son," he said, "whatever you resolve to do, avoid decisions on an empty stomach. You will stay for dinner and for the night. Tomorrow, if you still intend to pursue this, you may do so. In the meantime, this house is yours."

Montoya kept a frugal table, but mutton chops and chickpeas were served on majolica plates, and country wine in crystal goblets. For the first time since his departure from Padua, Miguel sat down to a quiet meal. It loosened the cramped exhaustion of his body and soul. The Montoyas, though eager to hear about his journey, did not press him with questions. After dinner Doña Soledad had his room readied.

"Go to sleep," Don Fernando said. "We shall talk in the morning."

The next day Miguel declared that he had decided to go to the house.

"Maybe you are right," Don Fernando agreed after his initial surprise. "Show them that here in Aragón we fight for what is ours. And if it comes to blows, then sell your skin as high as you can."

Miguel embraced the old man and kissed the hands of Doña Soledad, whose eyes were full of tears. Then he left the house.

The Montoyas stood on their balcony, watching him cross the square. They saw him walking up to the guards and saw the soldiers holding their halberds across the gate. Some words were apparently exchanged; then the two took Miguel between them and disappeared with him into one of the alleys leading away from the square.

Doña Soledad clung to her husband. "They will kill him," she said, sobbing.

Don Fernando shook his head. "I do not believe it," he said. "Talavera could have done away with him months ago, through an emissary, and seized the property. He did not do it, but went through the trouble of setting a trap. I think the old spider wants to groom the boy for his own purposes. But cheer up, Solita. If I have any eyesight, this wasp will tear up the net."

Through cobblestoned lanes, across sun-baked church squares, Miguel was led to the monastery of Saint Dominicus, which was the seat of the Inquisition's local chapter. His bodyguards brought him into the oratory, where Padre Domingo received fellow clerics and petitioners. The prior was known to be one of the fiercest members of his order. *Domini canes*, they called themselves, the Hounds of the Lord, ready to tear heresy to pieces. His appearance, however, belied this reputation, throwing off guard all those who had braced themselves to face a hollow-eyed fanatic. He was a portly monk who looked as if he were fond of good food and of pretty women in the confessional.

"Well, well" — he smiled as Miguel knelt before him — "here is the prodigal son. It took some effort to get you to come home." He gestured to Miguel to rise. "Before you take possession of your house," he went on, "I have instructions to take you with me to Toledo. His Eminence wants to make your acquaintance. We have a guest cell ready for you, where you may rest for a while until sunset. We shall take advantage of the coolness of the night for our travel."

n the roof of the Casa de los Reyes the banner of the Holy Office was raised at full staff, showing the picture of the Virgin and the Child against Toledo's blue sky. The cardinal was in residence.

In the Sala de los Moros — so called for the Moorish spoils displayed there, arms arrayed along the walls and tattered silken flags hanging from the cedar-beamed ceiling — Don Pedro was holding audience under an age-blackened crucifix that contrasted starkly with the heathenish splendor of the hall. He was about to receive the Bishop of Valencia, but had decided otherwise. Gil de Vega was called and ordered to set up another appointment for His Grace. Don Pedro wanted to collect his thoughts at some leisure before the arrival of the next visitor.

The evening before, when Padre Domingo reported to him that Miguel de Roxas had arrived in town, Don Pedro had merely acknowledged the information without asking the padre's opinion of the young man. This had slightly vexed the monk, for Padre Domingo flattered himself on being a sharp judge of character. Good breed, Your Eminence, he would have said. Good breed, but champing at the bit. Will have to be broken slowly, with patience.

The cardinal would not have minded this advice. He thought highly of patience.

*　*　*

There had been considerable speculation in Brussels when Pedro de Talavera, Chancellor Granvella's First Secretary, had unexpectedly entered the order of Saint Dominicus. Unrequited love for a Flemish girl, some had said. Others pretended to know that the young man had experienced a sudden spiritual revelation — an occurrence not infrequent in those times.

The rumors were not altogether unfounded. Talavera had indeed fallen in love with a girl from Ghent, and when that affection was not returned he found himself thinking of her for a longer time than his pride would suffer. He needed a change, and asked for a leave of absence to go to Italy. After two months' diversion, of sampling the joys the Peninsula offers the discriminating visitor, he felt that it was time to resume his duties at the chancellery.

In Brussels, however, another blow to his self-esteem awaited him: the man he had personally selected to be his substitute had been unmasked as a Calvinist spy. By the time the discovery was made, more than half of the Imperial dispatch code had been revealed to the German Protestant League. The remainder was safeguarded by the silence of a Spanish emissary at Nürnberg who had died on the rack, his tongue bitten through.

Pedro de Talavera had resigned from his post at once and taken the Three Vows. For a year he did extraordinary penitence, far harsher than the one prescribed by monastic rule. Tortured by self-doubt, he was obsessed by his failures. Sifting and resifting the events of his past, he detected in himself selfishness, impatience, arrogance, an inordinate love of life, and ruthless ambition.

As Imperial Secretary, living in the midst of decisions on the century's great conflicts, he used these as a fencing ground to sharpen his diplomatic skills, to learn his craft as a statesman. Thus, though a loyal Catholic, he had been dealing with the Protestants on a purely political plane, considering them no worse than the Emperor's other enemies, the Turks and the French, mere adversaries with whom a truce could be negotiated whenever the fortunes of war demanded it.

After the incident at Nürnberg, however, his wounded conscience prodded him to think again about the heretics. In his cell, between prayers, he reflected on them. Were they not brazenly pushing themselves between man and God — doing away with the anointed mediator, the priest? Did they not threaten the foundation of the throne, the True Faith? He saw the schism turn into strife, and strife into chaos. His duty was clear to him: self-punishment — fasts and flagellations — would not keep heresy at bay. It was necessary to become Christ's soldier and to crush the demon. His need to purge himself became one with the need to purge the Church. He sought permission to return to the world. This granted, King Philip had him take the rites of ordination, and appointed him to the Holy Office. Of superior intelligence, and spurning personal gain, Talavera rose in the hierarchy and in due time became the King's adviser in matters spiritual and secular alike.

A few years later King Philip obtained for him the red hat and made him the kingdom's Great Inquisitor.

Throughout Spain and Flanders the stakes were blazing. Don Pedro would make a point of presiding over the Act of Faith whenever it took place in Toledo, although lately it had become difficult for him. A sense of hideous futility would invade him as he sat on the dais, facing the wood-piles, a haggard figure in crimson, his heart cringing at the sights and sounds before his eyes. After such ceremonies, with the smell of burning flesh still clinging to his robes, he would throw himself on his knees before the Crucified One, begging Him to strengthen his faith, which now had passed the point of no return.

* * *

From a gold and ivory clock the ten minutes formerly allotted to the bishop were clicking off, one by one. The cardinal allowed curiosity to get the better of him. He was conducting an experiment, reckoning with an unknown quantity — the mind and soul of Juan de Roxas' son.

He touched a bell.

At the hall's opposite end, a red velvet curtain parted.

"Don Miguel de Roxas, Your Eminence," Gil de Vega announced, and retired, taking up his customary listening post near the door.

As his sight was growing weaker, it had become the cardinal's habit not to look at those whom he received in audience until they had walked the dozen steps from the entrance up to his seat. This time he strained his eyes to make out the appearance of his visitor, and felt a surge of pleasure.

Miguel now stood before Don Pedro, dropped to his knee, and kissed the hand of the cardinal, who motioned him to rise.

"I am pleased that you have come home."

"It was my duty, Your Eminence."

Miguel's voice betrayed none of the dread and diffidence he was sharing with those who, through the ages, have been summoned before a deputy of absolute power, but he could not keep his heart from pounding against his ribs.

"I knew your father, Miguel de Roxas, and I wish I could have prevented his rash deed."

The cardinal paused. He read the fearful question in Miguel's eyes.

(The padre, though chatting about everything under the sun during the journey, had not touched on Juan de Roxas or the manner of his death.)

"It was aconite," he said quietly. "Your father was wearing the vial on a chain around his neck."

Aconite. Through his fright and distress, Miguel felt a rush of relief. The substance killed almost instantly.

"Yes, I knew him quite well," Don Pedro went on, "years ago, during our student days at Salamanca. He was somewhat shy, as I recall, but of ready wit, and a delightful companion once you had gained his trust . . ."

He indicated a chair. Miguel complied with the unspoken command.

"He was uncommonly diligent and would even save his allowance to pay an old Jew for lessons in Arabic so that he could read Avicenna's work in the original text . . ."

Miguel's throat tightened. During the last vacation Juan de Roxas had brought forth some Arabic treatise on surgery and with mock gravity had pointed out a commentator's error, indicating that such pedants' triumphs were not to be taken too seriously.

"How old are you?"

"Nineteen years, Your Eminence."

"Of age, then." There was compassion in the cardinal's voice.

Tears welled up in Miguel's eyes. He yearned to fall on his knees, to bury his face in the folds of the red silk, to have the fine-boned hand stroke his hair. He set his teeth and fought off the weakness.

The cardinal observed him in silence. Then he asked, "Where is your mother?"

"She has been dead these twelve years."

"What was her name?"

"Marguerite Steen."

"The Steens from Ghent?"

"Yes, Your Eminence."

The cardinal's expression remained calm, as the memory of a sunny winter morning, long gone by, dazzled his eyes.

He was riding across the cathedral square in Ghent, accompanied by young Adrian van Buskirk, scion of one of the town's distinguished families and eager apprentice in the arts of statecraft and diplomacy.

Everywhere, bundled-up children were at play, laughing, shouting, pulling their little sleighs, and pelting each other with snowballs.

Passing by Banker Steen's house, he felt a stray missile hit him between the shoulder blades. Stunned, he quickly turned around and saw a girl of no more than sixteen years standing there, wrapped in a white woolen coat, blue eyes sparkling and cheeks aglow from the cold. Her hood had fallen back, revealing blond braids covered with ice needles.

"A hundred pardons, sir," she had called out to him. "It was meant for Adrian!"

The merry, unembarrassed apology had enchanted him, and his companion had acknowledged it by laughingly shaking his fist at her.

"Pieter Steen's granddaughter," Buskirk had said, still smiling, as they rode on. "The old man dotes on her. You can see why."

In the following weeks the Imperial Secretary had seen to it that he was formally introduced at the patrician's house. He began to court the girl. At first she tolerated him, then gently started to discourage him, and finally, one day, she told him straight out what he already guessed — that she could not see herself as Doña Marguerita de Talavera (rolling the *r*'s of the sonorous name, she had made it sound just a trifle too grand) and that she would never leave her homeland.

And yet, the cardinal reflected, first sorrowfully then wryly, she had come to wed a Spaniard, had gone over the Pyrenees with him, and had borne him a son.

Again, his eyes rested on Miguel.

There it was — somewhat lengthened — her short, straight nose; there were her deep blue eyes under dark brows, and, set off by high cheekbones, her generous, sensitive mouth. The body, slim, sinewy and long-legged, was solid and easy in the shoulders.

The cardinal smiled.

Spain and Flanders, he found, had done well by Miguel de Roxas.

"What are your plans?" he asked. "Will you continue your studies?"

"I intend to, Your Eminence."

"I am pleased. Now tell me, why medicine?"

"My father was a physician. I merely follow in his footsteps."

"How far along are you in your studies?"

37

"This is my second year, Your Eminence."

"Did your father influence you as to the choice of your subject?"

"No, Your Eminence. It was my own decision."

"Galen is outmoded in Padua, I am told." The cardinal smiled.

Miguel returned the smile.

"Not entirely, Your Eminence," he began, as if he were talking to a friend of his father's.

"So he is taught there even now?"

"Yes, Your Eminence, as far as his work on the bones is concerned. But his writing is no longer used as the sole anatomy text after it became clear that, as Your Eminence knows, Galen had dissected merely dogs and apes."

"Is that so?"

"Indeed, Your Eminence. Nobody bothers any longer to point out Galen's mistakes; they are obvious. It is in revealing and correcting the errors of the living that modern anatomy is coming into its own."

"Have you witnessed such instances?"

"I have, your Eminence."

"Tell me about them."

The exponents, young and old, of the young sciences needed close watching, the Holy Office had decreed, detecting a principle of rebellion in their insistence on proof wherever a new theory was being advanced. The cardinal kept abreast of their strides, but, owing to a curious spiritual mortification, he denied himself any intellectual pleasure from new discoveries, even after they had been accepted by the Church. It had not always been that way. There was a time when Pedro de Talavera,

Imperial Secretary and owner of a copy of *De humani corporis fabrica* — all volumes — with a handwritten dedication to him by the author, would often invite Vesalius to dinner and the two would talk the night away, speaking of sun, moon, and stars, of the wheels in the immense clockwork, and of that most enigmatic cosmos — the human body.

The cardinal listened to the young voice. He had thought those days were dead.

"There was the Procurator Contarini," Miguel said eagerly. (He had intended to tell the story to his father at the next vacation.) "For weeks he complained of headaches and was vomiting bile. He was treated for poison, but he died. At the request of the family, Acquapendente dissected him and found a blood clot on his brain the size of an egg. A few days later Ser Grillo, the mayor, fell sick, showing similar symptoms. Acqua—— I mean, Acquapendente, lost no time. He drilled open Grillo's skull, looked for the clot, found and removed it. Grillo recovered."

Don Pedro nodded.

"I envy you. You are allowed to learn from your mistakes. Contarini was expendable. I am not so fortunate, as I minister to the ailments of this kingdom. I have no margin for error. The autopsy would be on the dead body of Spain."

Don Pedro paused. He was aware of the possibility that the late Juan de Roxas, like so many misguided humanists, had looked on the Holy Office's ends and means with misgivings and that, if so, those views had been imparted to Miguel. So he took gentle steps and felt his way.

"Do you know," he asked, "that we have eighty thousand Marranos on our hands?"

The inclusive pronoun was intended to suggest to Miguel that he was being given a voice in the matter.

"I did not, Your Eminence."

The reply sounded apologetic. Now the cardinal had reached navigable waters.

"You were living abroad, absorbed by your studies," he allowed, "but the day has come for you to face our plight, as every Spaniard should do. The Holy Office has been accused of dealing harshly, even unjustly, with the New Christians. The charge is true."

Don Pedro could see that Miguel was thrown off balance by this unexpected admission and that he was striving to rally his thoughts. He gave him no time to do so.

"It is their misfortune to have been born in this century. Two hundred years ago the Church might have afforded them sufficient time for true conversion. These days there can be no such luxury. The Faith is beleaguered. The Marranos are the enemy within our walls. Your father shirked his duty when he refused his share of the common guilt which is the very mortar that binds together the groundstones of any kingdom in this world or the next. The Nazarene allowed the Innocent to be slain."

Slowly, almost involuntarily, Miguel nodded. He was unable to find the suspected flaw in this reasoning, yet was ashamed to surrender. How could his father have left him to deal with this cunning man? Why could he not be here to argue the point with the cardinal? Juan de Roxas would have been more than a match for the prelate. "Not bad," he would have said, "not bad at all. Of course, it holds no water." Miguel could hear the quiet voice with the hint of a gentle smile in it. It faded, leaving him wretched and spent. He must not let himself think of his father; not now, he told himself. It would break his strength, already weakened. He had had no breakfast that morning, having been unable to swallow a single bite at the Dominicans' refectory table. His stomach gave a turn, and part of him would have welcomed the fainting spell he felt approaching. Rocked by the flood and ebb of the blood in his temples, he grasped the arms of his chair and closed his eyes for an instant, only to force them open again. Every nerve alert, yet his face a mask of deferential attention, he awaited the cardinal's next move.

"Ours is a bitter calling," he heard the low voice again, "but we will talk about this sometime soon."

Fear stabbed through Miguel's heart. Was he not to go home? Why was the cardinal going to such lengths to justify to him the acts of the Holy Office? Why, after all, had the estate not been seized? *What price his house?* As for his father's guilt, he would sort that out later. (Innards first, went the dissection rule. They spoil. Bones can wait.)

Don Pedro touched a bell. The secretary brought in two rolls of parchment and a box. Then he withdrew.

"Miguel de Roxas," the cardinal said, "you have come back to claim your inheritance. The Crown has kept nothing back. Here are your father's testament and the keys to your house."

There was also a letter of credit. Probably thirty thousand escudos, Miguel thought. He had seen the sum mentioned in a copy of his father's will. But why not give it to him in gold? Was he supposed to spend his money in Spain? Luckily, there was still the Venetian account. Once in Italy, he calculated quickly, he only would have to go with the testament to the Mocenigo bank to touch the sum.

The cardinal had unfolded the paper.

"Here are fifty thousand escudos."

"Your Eminence — I possess a copy of the will. It mentions only thirty thousand."

"The twenty thousand have been converted from your father's Venetian assets."

Miguel did not allow himself to feel the blow. All his efforts went into concealing its impact.

The cardinal watched him.

"Where do you wish to continue your studies?" he asked. "At Salamanca? Alcalá? Or in your home town?"

His fright notwithstanding, Miguel felt insulted. After studying in Padua, he was to vegetate at a Spanish university, where they still believed in Adam's rib? At least he had the option to live at home.

"I shall go to Saragossa, Your Eminence."

"Good. There are still two weeks until the fall term. Time enough to settle in your house. After matriculation you will report to Padre Domingo from time to time. It will please me to be apprised of your progress."

As the cardinal offered his hand to his visitor to kiss, the ruby on his finger flashed a message to the young man. Miguel had to suppress a smile of triumph. His mother's jewelry! He would sell it as soon as he reached home — then two weeks to reach the border! He could not trust himself to look at the cardinal, feeling his eyes sparkling with defiance. So he lowered them and made the sign of the Cross.

Dismissed by Don Pedro, he withdrew.

As he passed through the antechamber, Gil de Vega bowed to him.

"Half an hour!" the secretary exclaimed, smiling. "Permit me to congratulate you, Don Miguel. The limit, so far, has been ten minutes. You must have found your way into His Eminence's good book."

For a moment, Miguel was puzzled. Why the gratuitous compliment? But then he shrugged; he had other preoccupations. He returned the bow and left the palace.

In the evening of that day Don Pedro received Padre Domingo at the charterhouse. After they had disposed of the current affairs, the monk summoned the courage to ask the cardinal about Juan de Roxas' son.

"Your Eminence thinks to have won?"

"No. He goes back to Saragossa. You will have an eye on him — sharp and invisible."

o the sound of the Ave bells, Doña Soledad was watering the flowers on her balcony when she heard approaching hoofbeats and the clattering of wheels on the square's cobblestones. A carriage appeared and stopped in front of the Roxas house. She saw Miguel alight from it, followed by a corpulent monk whom he was helping to descend. It was Padre Domingo. The latter said a few words to the soldiers, who saluted and marched away.

Miguel knelt, kissed the padre's hand, and was given a blessing by the monk, who then clambered back into the carriage and was borne off. He brought forth a key, inserted it into the huge, artfully wrought iron lock, and turned it. The gate opened; Miguel entered and closed it behind him.

Doña Soledad stared at the door behind which he had disappeared. Then she sought Don Fernando. After they had exhausted many conjectures, she begged her husband to go to Miguel.

"No, Solita," he answered. "It will be up to him to come here. We must wait to see whether he still knows his friends."

Miguel had locked the front door from the inside. He passed through the hall into the patio and sat down on the

44

rim of the well. It seemed to him that he was still hearing the clatter of the wheels and, through it, the comfortable conversation of Padre Domingo, who had declared himself enchanted to have a scholar from Padua as a traveling companion, to talk about everything under the sun, "from the cedar to the hyssop."

By and by, the quiet of the patio silenced the hammering inside his head. For the past three weeks he had been in the company of one of his father's murderers, making small talk, suspended in a bubble of absurdity. Every single day, from dawn till dusk, he had been on his guard against any careless word, any gesture that might betray his innermost thoughts.

The monk, on the other hand, had enjoyed himself. Shielded by his Mother Church, which held the slaying of clerics punishable by fire, he had not even bothered to have the young man's dagger confiscated.

Miguel tore off his clothes and kicked them across the patio in helpless rage. Aside from the sweat and dust of the journey, they had, he felt, been soiled by the padre's touch whenever the rattling carriage had thrown its passengers against each other.

He lowered the bucket into the well, hauled it up, and poured the cold water over himself, three, four, five times. It made him gasp — the first deep breaths he had drawn in a long while. Dripping, he crossed the patio and mounted the stairs. His sense of decorum protested against his nakedness, but he silenced it. Was it not his house? His house in which to do as he pleased? His house.

In his room nothing was amiss except the dried crocodile he had brought home from a Paduan apothecary shop on his last vacation. It must have taken the fancy of the

Inquisition soldiers — the two pieces of string that had held it suspended were still dangling from the ceiling. Yet his books — mostly medical treatises — had not been touched, nor had his coats and doublets in the closet. In his trunk his shirts and underclothes were neatly stacked, exhaling a smell of coarse soap, sun-dried stones, and cedarwood. He dressed and passed into his mother's quarters.

Since the day Juan de Roxas' wife had been carried away by a sudden illness, nothing had been changed there. The canopied four-poster bed in which she had died, her lute, her lace-making pillow, her embroidery frame holding a half-finished canvas with the threaded needle still pinned on a stitch — all seemed to proclaim that Marguerite de Roxas had merely gone on a journey and would return any day. Yet despite Paca's fervent care of the room, Miguel had always known that his mother would never come back.

In a way, her sudden disappearance had come as no surprise to her small son, for deep in his heart he had always believed her to be a visitor from a realm of legend who had only followed a whim to dwell with mortals for a while.

Her blond hair flying, she would gather her cotton skirts (at home she had no use for the modish steel corsets and triangle robes) and run through the house on such nimble feet that the wooden stairs emitted hardly a creak.

Yet she had come from a stock of solid Flemish burghers. The Steens of Ghent were wealthy merchants, devoted to the Emperor. Charles had liked old Pieter Steen, the shrewdest broker in town. Whenever he was holding court in Ghent — where he was born — the Emperor would send for the old man or even grace the Steens with an informal visit. Among his suite was Juan de Roxas, his physician, and before long the doctor had won the heart of Marguerite, Pieter Steen's eighteen-year-old granddaughter.

Miguel carried a chair to the bed, climbed on it, and, extending his arm over the canopy, felt for the object he knew to be lying in the center of the taut velvet.

"There is no safer place for keys," Marguerite, the merchant's daughter, had laughingly maintained. "Thieves get into closets, under beds. They claw through chests and drawers; they bend and crouch. It never occurs to them to look up and above their heads for things to steal."

Having found what he wanted, Miguel jumped down and went over to a certain tapestry. He lifted it, uncovering a wall cabinet. Unlocked, it revealed a silver-mounted box of sandalwood. As he took it out, it felt sickeningly light. Even before he set it down on the table he knew that it was empty. Not altogether empty, however. On the green velvet cushion there lay a message written in a clerk's meticulous hand, stating that on instructions of His Eminence, Don Pedro de Talavera, Great Inquisitor of the Kingdom of Castile and Aragón, all jewelry owned by the late Doña Marguerita de Roxas had been sent to the Shrine of the Virgin at the cathedral to be displayed on the Blessed Statue until such time as Miguel de Roxas, son and lawful heir of the deceased, would enter the state of holy matrimony, in which case the said Miguel de Roxas would be authorized to claim his heirloom for his wedded wife.

The paper bore the seal of the Holy Office and was signed by Gil de Vega, secretary to His Eminence. A list of sixteen pieces was enclosed.

Still holding the key, Miguel stood motionless, hardly

registering the loss of the jewelry, paralyzed as he was by the ease with which the cardinal had outguessed him. Evidently Don Pedro had sent this Vega to Saragossa within minutes after the audience. The secretary must have traveled on winged feet, overtaking Padre Domingo's lumbering coach, in order to seize the pieces before their owner's arrival. But then — his heart stood still — then Vega must have a key to the house! He spun around as if he were being watched from behind. There was nobody. Suddenly feeling the need to have his back protected, he retreated from the center of the room until his shoulders touched the wall. His overworked senses made him hear footsteps approaching from the patio balcony — or did they mount the stairs? As soon as he listened the sounds would fade. Was the entrance gate bolted? No. Moving toward the door, he passed onto the balcony. Only half of the patio was drenched in moonlight. Keeping in the black shadow, Miguel gained the winding stairs. He began to descend, but despite his overcautious advancing, or perhaps because of it, he missed his footing and twisted his ankle. The sharp pain shattered the rigidity of his fear. Calling himself a craven fool, he felt his way toward the gate and drew the heavy bolt across it. Then he made his way into the kitchen in search of flintstones, touchwood, and candles, which he found with the help of the moonrays falling on the hearth. He struck fire and lighted a taper. Shielding the flickering flame with his hand, he went back upstairs and into his bedroom. He closed the door and pulled the heaviest chest against it. Then he took two pistols from a drawer, assured himself that they were loaded, and threw himself, fully clothed, on his bed, the weapons on a chair beside him. He intended to stay awake through the night, but fatigue won over.

At first he sank into dreamless depths. Then he found himself wandering at nighttime through a maze of narrow alleys in search of a particular street. In and out the dark, winding lanes he went. Some of them led to dead ends, making him retrace his steps. He tried to question the passersby, shadowy shapes of children and old men, but they all hurried past him, dissolving into the darkness. At last a small boy pointed to a windowless house crouching against the city wall. Was this his father's prison?

"Knock there."

He pounded at the door. There was no sound. But when he threw himself once more against the splintering gate, he heard the blow echoing through the alley. Encouraged, he listened. Suddenly the poundings redoubled, accompanied by shouts. "Miguel! Miguel! It's me! Open, for the sake of Jesus!"

He woke up, his head spinning. Daylight filled the room. Someone, at the height of impatience, it seemed, was now hurling stones against the front gate. He ran downstairs, pulled back the bolt, and opened the gate on a short, round woman with graying hair pulled back into a substantial bun, and a network of tiny wrinkles around her jet-black eyes. She was carrying a basket containing eggs, peppers, a jug of olive oil, a loaf of bread, and a fresh-killed chicken. She put it down and threw her arms around Miguel.

"I came as soon as they told me that you were back, dear," she panted. "What misfortune!"

Paca seemed unchanged. Picking up her foodstuffs, she preceded him into the kitchen.

"Paca, what happened? What do you know?"

"All in good time, Miguel. First let me cook you something to eat. The padre said you had no supper."

"Damn the padre! Paca, what happened?"

"I don't know too much."

"Tell me what you know. Also — where have *you* been?"

"At the Carmelites. When they — sealed the house, the padre had me summoned and told me that I had to stay at the convent until they had word from you. They had me scrubbing floors there . . . now where is my tinderbox?"

She found it and busied herself at the hearth. Soon eggs and green peppers were frying in an iron skillet. Miguel kept silent and let her work.

The sun-filled kitchen with its familiar, garlic-dominated smells, gave him for a few moments the illusion that nothing whatever had happened since he had watched Paca making her town-famous *chorizos* during his last vacation. Indeed, nothing had been touched. The copper pans hung from the blackened rafters; the majolica plates stood on their shelves. When he was a child, the kitchen had been his delight, with its huge fireplace, its sink, whose blue-green tiles echoed those on the outer house wall, and its beams festooned with garlands of peppers, onions, and garlic. The rush-bottomed chairs around the table had seen much service, and so had the table itself, its scrubbed top showing the scars of years of bread-cutting.

Paca set before him a plate heaped with steaming food and took a chair.

"Now, Miguel," she said, "this is what happened. The evening of Pentecost, in the dead of the night, your father let in two men, all wrapped and cowled. They talked for a while in the study. Afterward, he came down to me and said, 'Paca, we will have to put a few people in the cellar, just for one night. Make sure that they have food and some blankets.' I didn't like it one bit and said so. 'Don Juan,' I said, 'you'll get yourself into a mess of troubles, and all for those wretched Christ-killers.' 'Paca,' he said, 'don't be silly. They are three old men and a woman with a baby. And they will be gone in no time.' So they came, but I was suspicious, for I thought I knew two of them, but I couldn't put my finger on them.

"Well, the next day your father had to go to court — some Jews had killed a Christian child, and he had to look at the body of the poor little thing to say that they had stabbed it. What happened then, I don't know. They came for those in the cellar, took them away to the bonfires."

"The baby too . . . ?"

"No, not him, or the mother either. They took him away from her, though, to be christened. She screamed something terrible. So they said that if she converted, she could see the boy again in ten years."

Miguel pushed his plate away.

"And . . ."

"Your father never came back from court. The same afternoon they sealed the gate and sent me to the nuns. The next days, there was much talk there, for all their rule of silence, and they said that your father . . ." Paca looked at her hands.

". . . had killed himself?"

"Yes," she whispered.

"It's true, Paca."

She crossed herself.

"Miguel, what will you do? You won't go away again, will you?"

The arrival of old Maria Luz, the laundress, spared him from answering. He left the kitchen and went to his father's study.

The key was in the lock. The young man's hands did not tremble as he turned it, but they felt weak, as if the light task were beyond their strength. The door opened almost against his will. He stood on the threshold, peering into the semidarkness within. Through the closed shutters thin shafts of sunlight were stealing, allowing his eyes to make out familiar objects one by one: the oaken desk with globe and astrolabe on it, the Vesalian skeleton sitting on a chair in a corner, the books on the shelves, the two portraits on the dark-paneled wall that had looked down on him from childhood, Marguerite drawn by Clouet, and the Emperor sketched by Titian.

He walked over to the window, threw it open, turned around, and faced the room. Juan de Roxas' absence hung over it like an unresolved chord.

Miguel sat down in the dead man's chair at the desk, his forehead in his hand.

What had happened and why had it happened?

"A correct post-mortem diagnosis," Acquapendente used to say, "depends to a considerable degree on our knowledge of the deceased one's way of life. More often than not such evidence will show you that it was inevitable that he met precisely the kind of death he did."

The deceased one's way of life . . . It had been quiet and withdrawn from the world. Juan de Roxas, these last years, had lived with his books and his flowers, measuring time by his son's school terms and vacation visits. Why had he been called, he and not the town physician, to testify in this mock trial? Had he made himself suspect to the Holy Office? How?

As far as he knew, his father had had no truck with any Jew except long ago, in Salamanca, with that old scribe (the one the cardinal had mentioned) who had taught him Arabic and once had rescued him from a tight spot. But that was more than forty years ago and the man, even then, had been in his seventies.

So what about those four in the cellar? What had made them so important as to cost his father's life?

So far, Miguel had never bothered his head about any Marranos. A fleeting, somewhat exasperated compassion (couldn't they run away?) was all they had ever elicited from him, his security bolstered by the flawlessness of the Roxas family tree, which had been free of any Jewish, Moorish, or Converso strain for over six generations according to a ponderous certificate.

"To each age its folly," his father used to say, as Miguel recalled now. "Could every Roxas trust his wife while he was away fighting some Saracens? Still, the sheepskin has its use. It keeps those *Domini canes* off your back."

All the same, they had attacked and murdered his father, pedigree or not. Whoever had set the trap must have known Juan de Roxas well enough to surmise that the doctor would refuse to bear his "burden of common guilt," as the cardinal had called it. Guilt toward those Jews? What sin had his father been expected to commit against them? Quickly, Miguel thought through the Ten Commandments. The first four did not apply. The Fifth, Sixth, and Seventh almost made him laugh. The Eighth and Ninth? Absurd. The Tenth? *Thou shalt not bear false witness against thy neighbor.*

Well, they could hardly be called the Roxas' neighbors. No Jew was ever seen near the Square San Isidro. They lived in the ghetto, the Juderia; they even had to observe a curfew. At dusk you could spot a few of them near the city walls, passing like bats . . . Bats. The feared monsters of Monna Aldruda. Why, those Jews did not kill Christian children any more than her "vampires" sucked blood. Did it follow, then, that the King was as foolish as the old woman had been? Or were there further reasons for the ceaseless manhunt? What was it about the beleaguered Faith? Beleaguered by those shadowy, frightened creatures?

Miguel ruefully remembered that he had lately avoided talking politics with his father, because at the mere mention of the King the older man would stare straight ahead, as if beholding the ship of state lurching ahead, its helm in Philip's inept and rigid hands.

Bored by such brooding — Spanish matters concerned him but little, since he was bent on an Italian career — Miguel had quickly discovered how to smooth his father's furrowed brow. All he had to do was steer the talk away from Spain and toward Padua. He wished that he had listened to his father more carefully, for now, ill prepared and alone, he had to confront some frightening questions.

What was it that King Philip had said recently? That he would rather rule over Catholic ruins than over a prosperous heretic land? Miguel had always considered himself a faithful son of the Church, but his common sense bristled against such a proposition. Catholic ruins — Philip certainly was seeing to it that Spain fitted that description. He was destroying the Marranos to clean the kingdom of all seeds of heresy. Yet Spain, Juan de Roxas had once said, would not be purer after this bloodletting; only poorer.

If thine eye offends thee, pluck it out.

But damn and hellfire, those New Christians, peasants and tradesmen for the greater part, were not Spain's eyes; they were her hands! The old duke had been right. Fields were lying fallow; houses were slowly crumbling. And had not Paca complained recently that some broken tiles in the kitchen sink could not be replaced, since there was nobody left of those Mudejar potters who knew how to make them?

No doubt, the King was out of his mind. Was it not to be expected? Miguel recalled that his father had one day told him of a visit to old Queen Juana, Philip's grandmother. Juan de Roxas had accompanied the Emperor to the castle of Tordesillas, where they found the old woman sitting on a bare floor strewn with dead birds and talking to the ghost of her husband.

"They need some fresh blood in the House of Austria," his father had said. "Look at Don Juan, for example . . ."

But Don Juan was excluded from the succession, although he was the Emperor's son: his mother had been a mere innkeeper's daughter. Philip was the legitimate ruler, who believed that the kingdom's welfare had to be achieved through fire and sword. So, apparently, did the cardinal, who was not demented. The emaciated face rose before Miguel, not with the expression of sympathy and winning urbanity he had seen, but as aggrieved and cruel as Hell itself. And he understood: *the Cardinal knew better.*

What, then, did Don Pedro want of him, Miguel de Roxas? He strove to recall the audience in Toledo, to remember every word that was spoken. There was gentleness at the outset, which had lured him into lowering his defenses. Lured — that was the right word. Lured, the way Sir Halewyn . . . For years, he had not thought of the gruesome tale with which Grandmother Steen had tried to scare him into good behavior, a six-year-old on a visit to Ghent with his parents. To impress her little grandson, she had changed the Flemish Bluebeard into a child-killer who would sing sweetly to any wild-running and disobedient boy, making his victim follow him into the woods, where he would pluck out the little one's heart, for Sir Halewyn had given his own heart to the Devil and needed a fresh one every so often to keep alive.

The story had not served its purpose at the time. Young Miguel (to his father's quiet amusement) had merely asked how the fiend had managed to survive the exchanges; but, strangely enough, it frightened him now. He saw a long, slender hand emerge from a sleeve of flowing red silk, reaching out to pluck — not the heart — but the soul from him. The cardinal needed a fresh and young one for his own, which was worn and damned.

Enough, he told himself. He could not afford to dwell on those fancies if he wanted to keep a clear head. Perhaps it would help if he went for a walk.

San Isidro's tower cast a short, black shadow that barely cooled the heat-baked cobblestones of the deserted little square. Only a blind beggar sat on the church steps, asking for alms in a high-pitched singsong.

Passing close by the wretch, Miguel dropped a coin into the cupped, shriveled hand.

"God reward you, señor."

56

As he took the narrow lane leading to the city wall, he could not keep himself from looking back. The beggar was still sitting at the same spot.

Farther away from the square the street became crowded. Miguel threaded his way through a throng of monks, priests, soldiers, tattered urchins, water carriers, and beggars. For the first time he noticed the idleness of this crowd in a street that lacked the sights, sounds, and smells of the crafts — the dyer's vat, the blacksmith's hammer, the tanner's bark — so inseparable from Padua's populous quarters.

He reached the wall and climbed the hornwork. From there, one could look out across the Ebro Valley, over the foothills of the Sierra de Alcubierre to the snowy peaks of the Pyrenees in the distance. Miguel, however, wasted no time appreciating the view. He was studying the terrain.

On three sides, east, south, and west, Saragossa was protected by ramparts, their gates manned night and day. Toward the north the Ebro provided a second moat, over which the stone bridge crossed in seven buttressed arcs. Its head on the left bank was also guarded. Padre Domingo was doubtlessly kept informed about the comings and goings through the bridge gate.

The town was already milling with students, although the fall term was still a few weeks off. With any luck, Miguel thought, he might mingle with a strolling group of them and thus pass through the gate. This obstacle cleared, he would have to head straight for the mountains; the road to Barcelona was too long.

What about swimming the Ebro at night? Impractical. The current was swift with strong eddies; God knew where he would be thrown ashore. Besides, he would have to do it with his clothes on, and his water-filled boots alone could drag him under.

His eyes measured the distance from the bridge to the foothills. How many miles to the mountains?

"My reverence, Don Miguel," someone said behind him. He turned around. The voice, like a smell, was recognizable at once, even after thirteen years.

"Why, Camacho."

"The same, Your Grace. My, my, how great oaks grow out of little acorns!"

The grin of the skeleton in Juan de Roxas' study was endearing compared to the smile that bared Camacho's yellow teeth. He had been employed in the Roxas household for a few months as a general servant, mostly at Paca's entreaty, because he was a distant relative of hers. Sly and handy, he had a way with women, but was detested by children in spite of his clever hands, which could whittle astonishing toys out of any old piece of wood. One day he had disappeared after a short conversation with Juan de Roxas, part of which young Miguel, listening at the door to his father's study, had overheard.

"If Doña Marguerita has dismissed you, Camacho," Juan de Roxas had said, "there is nothing I can do about it."

Camacho had left with his just earnings in his pockets and a few trinkets that had also found their way into them.

That evening Juan de Roxas had asked Marguerite why she had decided to dispense with Camacho's services.

"Prophylactic measure," she had answered, having picked up quite a few terms of the trade as the wife of a medical man.

It appeared that one of the Montoyas' scullery maids had

given birth to a boy. That in itself was nothing out of the ordinary, but the girl had shown a curiously burned hand. When the hour came, Doña Soledad had gone up to the servants' quarters and had assisted her. Between labor pains, the girl had sobbed out her story: Camacho had held her hand into a candle flame until she swore not to reveal his part in her plight. Paca at the time had a sixteen-year-old niece helping in the kitchen, and Marguerite feared a similar fate for her.

Miguel looked at the man without pleasure. The sallow face with the long, thin lips was lined by vice rather than by the years. The gaunt body was still stooped in the crooked way Miguel remembered.

"And how are you getting by, Camacho?" he heard himself say.

"The only way a beadle can get by in this town."

He pointed to a little church whose only bell was hanging motionless from a beam in its towerlet.

"There are few funerals — Saragossa has healthful air — a couple of weddings and sufficient christenings. The Aragonese are stingy."

He chose not to mention certain tokens of appreciation he had recently received from Padre Domingo for pertinent intelligence.

Miguel, to avoid further conversation, handed him a silver coin. Camacho shoved it into his pocket.

"Many thanks, Don Miguel. And if you will allow me to repay you, then take my advice. Stay out of mischief. The padre's arm has grown rather long these last weeks. But if you want to make a bolt for out there" — he indicated the north with his head — "then address yourself to me. For a modest fee I sometimes serve as a guide to those who desire to leave the kingdom. I know the footpaths and the hours when the bridge guard changes."

"That must make a tidy little side income, Camacho, what with all those Jews . . ."

"There are not too many of them left, Don Miguel. Before the trial and your father's — misfortune — they felt rather secure, having had some privileges in the Kingdom of Aragón. They thought the ill wind would blow over, that it would be enough to lie low for a while, that nothing was ever eaten as hot as it was cooked . . . Well, they have found out by now that they are to eat it even hotter. The padre will see to that. Don Juan, by the way — God rest his soul — might have saved himself and you a lot of trouble had he simply done what was asked of him."

Miguel nodded cautiously.

"All he had to do was to testify that the boy had been stabbed right there in the Jews' house. A pure formality."

"Was that not so?" Miguel asked, trying to keep his voice casual. The man, he sensed, was eager to flaunt his cleverness, his intimacy with the authorities, before his former master.

Camacho gave him a crafty look. "Evidence was needed. A Christian child — uncircumcised. It did not take much looking — my poor sister had a brood of nine. Two fistfuls of sand in his throat, no noise, and the body dropped into the Jews' house, with the proper stabs and the blood where it was needed and nowhere else. Don Juan had no business looking into the boy's mouth. Still, I think he would have kept his counsel had not those Jews been found in his cellar."

Miguel wasted no time at being horrified by Camacho.

He merely accepted the tale as another link in the chain of events that had led to his father's death.

"The padre had Masses read for the little martyr, and my sister has one less mouth to feed, so things are well all around. When I say 'all around,' of course, I am excepting your father and Don Gil. It was his idea to call Don Juan and not the town physician as an expert, because he had — still has — an eye on your house. He could not have known that the Eminence would develop a soft spot for you. My reverence, Don Miguel."

Noting with satisfaction the effect his story had on Miguel, he bowed and was gone.

The chicken legs sizzled in the iron skillet. Cheeks aglow, Paca busied herself at the hearth, preparing Miguel's first "Christian" meal. How thin he was, the poor orphan! And what misfortune!

She had always thought that his father had it coming to him, always reading those Arabic sheepskins, rarely going to church, having visitors from abroad, men passing through Saragossa and speaking ungodly languages who would call on Don Juan and be received with great civility. The business with the Jews had been the last straw.

Well, she would see to it that Miguel stayed out of mischief. Had she not promised Doña Marguerita to look after him? Could she ever forget how the dear young creature's hands had reached out for hers and had held them in a fever-hot clasp? "You will stay with them, Paca, won't you?"

The voice was dry and hoarse. Paca had merely nodded, amidst streaming tears. Had not her wrists shown the finger marks of the dying woman's grip, days after they had carried Doña Marguerita away in her coffin?

Grimly, she turned the chicken. There won't be any nonsense, she swore to herself. Miguel was to study at Saragossa, the padre had told her; he was to live at home. No foreigners to visit *him*. In due time he would get married. She could hardly wait to cradle his first son. Would that child have Miguel's blue eyes if he brought home a Spanish girl?

The entrance gate creaked, startling her from her speculations.

Miguel slowly ate his gazpacho, savoring every spoonful. Paca was hovering over him, eager for praise.

"Cold enough?" she asked.

The soup tureen had been cooling in the well for the last three hours. He nodded, attempting a smile with his mouth full.

"I'll have to fatten you up a little," she said.

He swallowed. "But, Paca, one fattens the calf, not the prodigal son."

Tears welled up in her eyes. Paca, though strong-minded, was "born near the water," as the Aragonese peasants put it. "The Holy Virgin be thanked that you are here."

Her joy suddenly made the food stick in his throat. "What would you have done if I had not come back?" he asked, trying to sound merely curious. "Where would you have gone?"

"I don't know. Doña Soledad would have taken me in, I suppose. She said so when they — sealed the house, before they took me away to the sisters. I would not have minded working for her . . . But what are you talking about? Don't you get it into your head to run away, Miguel de Roxas. We have had enough trouble here."

She changed his plate and brought forth the fried chicken pieces, a bowl of olives, dark bread, and a bottle of Rioja. "And why have you not yet called on Don Fernando?"

Why indeed? His brain refused to rationalize, to justify his acts and omissions. He kept silent, attacking the chicken with a vengeance, but sipping the wine cautiously.

"You should go over there," she insisted. "Otherwise, they will think you had no upbringing."

"Later, Paca." He sighed.

A sudden weariness came over him. Was it caused by the heat of the Spanish afternoon? He thanked Paca, and went up to his room. After closing the shutters, he took off his clothes, stretched out on the bed, and sank into the soothing depths of the siesta.

Camacho was trimming the candles before the altar of Santa Tecla, reflecting on his encounter — not entirely fortuitous — with Miguel de Roxas. The matter required careful thought, for his own interests were not easily protected in this complicated affair.

The young man obviously was contemplating flight. There was no mistaking the way his eyes had attempted to gauge the distance between the walls of Saragossa and the mountains. As a candidate for ransom, then, he needed watching.

Camacho preferred to overtake his prospects some five or six miles beyond the city wall, at the moment when they thought that they had escaped unnoticed. After relieving them of their last ten or twenty escudos by threatening to send the *Domini canes* after them, he would let them stumble on toward the mountains. In Miguel de Roxas' case, however, Camacho had two options, because of the conflicting interests of his two intermittent employers, Padre Domingo and Gil de Vega.

He put aside his trimming shears and paced up and down the short aisle.

If he brought back the fugitive within twelve hours, it would gain him the padre's favor, along with a small reward. At the same time, he would incur Don Gil's displeasure. If, on the contrary, he ransomed the young man, the financial gain would be greater. With the padre none the wiser, Don Gil, assured of the disappearance of the last Roxas, would be pleased.

Camacho had a great deal of admiration for Don Gil, for the patient guile the secretary had shown as he laid siege to Juan de Roxas' house. Vega, deeming it too dangerous, had avoided denouncing the doctor for conniving with Marranos; one does not accuse a royal physician of such a misdeed without proof. How much cleverer was it to summon him to court under the pretext of seeking his expert advice in this murder case, thus making the Holy Office sharply aware of his existence. In due time a man like Roxas would make himself suspect merely by his way of life, and his doom would be of his own doing. It had happened even sooner than Camacho had anticipated. But how had Don Gil known about the Jews in Roxas' cellar? This bit of information had evidently allowed the secretary to have the court cleared before the doctor could make his implied accusation in public.

There had been no opportunity for a long private audience with Vega; the latter had departed for Toledo right after the trial. Patience, Camacho told himself. Someday

Don Gil, back in town and ensconced in Roxas' house, would be in a condescending and expansive mood, ready to satisfy his servant's curiosity.

He took up his shears again and went to the little side altar, where he cut the wicks of the candles burning before a miraculous picture of Saint Jude, intercessor in difficult matters.

Miguel awoke at the ringing of the Vesper bells, conscious of a subtle fragrance he had breathed while asleep. A bowl filled with grapes and anise pastries was on the night stand. There was also a pitcher of wine and a silver goblet. Wryly, he looked at the food, the silent pleading of Paca's solicitude beginning to irritate him. Still, he took one of the cakes. It melted in his mouth. Then he pulled off a grape. Its sweet juice complemented the bitter flavor of the anise. Better stay away from the wine, though, he thought. No wonder the Jews were said to be abstinent. On their guard day and night, they could not allow themselves to get drunk.

So had he to be on guard, for that matter, ever since that day in Toledo. Why, in the Devil's name, could his father not have let well enough alone? Those Jews were as good as burned, no matter how absurd the charges against them, how contrived the evidence. Juan de Roxas had attempted to protect the unprotectable. His reward had been death, and now exile was awaiting his son. If he returned to the university, Miguel understood, he could never again come home. Yes, Padua would be exile; he would have to make a place for himself there among the less fortunate. Before, he had been a guest in good standing. From now on, he would be a fugitive.

He thought of past homecomings.

Alerted by the banging of the heavy door knocker, his father would hurry down from his study, followed by the beaming Paca. After the first affectionate greetings the two men would sit down in the patio while Paca would outdo herself in the kitchen. There would be conversations way into the night, during which he would relate the goings-on at Padua to Juan de Roxas, who listened in comfortable silence except when he threw in a question from time to time to assure Miguel of his deepest attention. There would be rides into the Gallego Valley, where the Roxas family owned an orchard. The older villagers would marvel at the young man, whom they had known as a child and whose golden-haired, spirited mother they had loved.

Miguel closed his eyes and listened to the voices of the past. They seemed to whisper to him from the very walls. A thought stirred in him. He watched it rise in uneasy fascination.

What if he complied?

Then he could keep his home. All he had to do was attend the University of Saragossa. True, he would have to listen with a straight face to assertions that the sky was made of copper or that on Doomsday man would rise from the sesamoid bone of his little finger like a stalk from a bean. What else?

Sardonically, his conscience began to reel off some other duties. He would have to do obeisance to the padre every fortnight. There would be frequent journeys to Toledo. Soon he might be asked to declare in court that those pitiful Jews were stabbing Christian children whenever nobody was looking. He would be told to report on certain suspects, Don Fernando de Montoya, for example. The latter assignment, however, might prove difficult to carry out, as the old warrior would be bound to forbid him his door.

There would be no more rides to the orchard. The peasants, a proud lot who resented the curtailing of their old privileges, suspected the Holy Office of being behind those efforts. They also had been fond of his father. How could he ever show his face there? Paca's inventive pampering would have to make up for both Montoya's contempt and the villagers' scorn.

Suddenly he laughed, as he had not laughed in many weeks.

"Class! Every cure" — he could almost hear Acquapendente pontificate — "every cure has its accompanying problems. You merely have to ascertain that they do not outweigh its benefit. Refrain from imitating King Darius' physician, who recommended decapitation against headache."

His laughter ended in a sigh of relief and of acceptance. To keep the house would have cost him his soul. It was too dear, if one remembered that at this price even the whole world was considered a bad bargain in certain quarters. The house might as well burn down with everything in it.

Miguel could almost see flames licking at his father's books. The Aldine *Odyssey*, its pages shriveling up, one by one, leaving a little heap of gray ashes . . . Marguerite's lute, burning with a crackling sound and bursting . . . The fire now had seized the balcony and the eaves of cedarwood . . . the roof collapsed, sending a long spray of sparks toward the night sky . . .

He shook himself, wrenching his mind from those fearful

yet strangely satisfying visions. He needed a clear head to see him through this ordeal.

He jumped up from the bed, dressed, and began pacing the room. An unnoticed escape called for money. Since his expenses were being watched by the Holy Office, he could remove only a small, unimportant sum from the town treasurer on his letter of credit. His mother's jewelry had been seized. He found it hard to believe that the house, even though it had been thoroughly searched, would not yield some valuables. Perhaps those *Domini canes* had overlooked a few trinkets, coins, or credit letters? What about his father's desk? Its secret drawer? Not so secret, though; it did not even have a key. One merely had to press down a spring under the table top to open it.

He left his room and went to the study.

The spring, somewhat hardened, released the drawer no more than a few inches. Miguel squeezed his hand into the opening. His outstretched fingers touched several pieces of paper, which he cautiously hauled out. They were tied together with a string.

His eager eyes fell on his own handwriting. Juan de Roxas had used the drawer to hold his son's correspondence.

Dejected, Miguel looked at the small bundle of pages. He knew that he should be touched by the value his father had put on those often carelessly penned letters, but his disappointment was acute. Was there truly nothing else in the drawer? The spring screeched, but he pulled out the drawer another inch and again forced his hand inside. This time his fingertips reached paper thicker than the letters he had sent from Padua. Vellum, perhaps? He clawed at the bulky rim with the nail of his middle finger, and slowly, after it had slipped away several times, he brought forth a rectangle of stiffish paper folded several times and showing a broken seal.

Doctissimo Amico, Johanni de Roxas, Protomedico S. Imp. Mai. Caroli Quinti glor. mem. et S. Reg. Mai. Philippi Sec. salutes, he read in a cursive script that had sprouted some spikes and prongs under an obviously German quill.

Who was this man who addressed Juan de Roxas as his friend? He looked at the signature, but could not decipher it. The Spanish night, duskless and sudden, had filled the room. Miguel went for light. When he entered the kitchen, Paca made him sit down for dinner. He obeyed, amazed by his own patience. He finished his meal and chatted with her for good measure. Then he took his candlestick and wished her good night. She heard him mount the winding staircase, but instead of going to his room he locked himself in his father's study.

She shook her head, suddenly uneasy.

The flickering candlelight fell on the page.

Greetings to my most learned friend, Juan de Roxas, Miguel read again, *former physician to His Late Imperial Majesty Charles V of glorious memory and to His Royal Majesty Philip II.*

I received your Vita on Pentecost Day and thank you most heartily for it. I shall be proud to incorporate it into my SPECULUM SCIENTIAE. *The proofs should be ready by mid-August. Next April the volume will go forth from my press, a tribute to our century's men of science who have added so significantly to our knowledge of the Creator's work and also — let it be hoped — a rewarding financial venture.*

It is with regret that I learn of your resolve to remain in retirement, but I console myself with the thought that your son, studying at Padua and raising his father's brightest hopes, will continue your life's work.

I extend my devoted regards to you, and may they be mutual.

Bartholomaeus Faber
Printer and Bookseller
at Basel
Kalendis maii
Anno Dom. MDLXXX

Miguel sat still, chin in palm, his eyes following the dancing shadows on walls and ceiling.

Faber in Basel! He knew the name; his father had often mentioned the printer when he was talking of things past. Juan de Roxas had even suggested that his son pay a call on that friend of many years — Basel was only a week's journey from Padua — but Miguel had been in no hurry to cross the Alps just to visit an old fogy, so he had let the matter rest.

He now wondered about this man for whom his father had written an account of his life for publication. Faber evidently had succeeded in coaxing such an endeavor from that recluse who, so far, had shared his memories with only his son and a few close friends — and then but sparingly. Miguel was somewhat familiar with his father's youth and his career at the Emperor's itinerant court. But what about recent events? Suddenly he realized that he had not seen his father for almost a year. Maybe the Vita mentioned some new facts that would explain what happened? What was behind this public account, which seemed at odds with Juan de Roxas' customary reticence? Who could tell? But one thing seemed certain: the answers, if there were any, lay in Basel.

Miguel went to the bookshelf, took down a heavy atlas, an *Orbis Pictus*, and spread it open on the desk. Green, red, and brown, EUROPA emerged from a pale blue Mediterranean, peopled with nymphs and Tritons. (The outer Atlantic showed merely a few spouting whales.) The Alps were indicated by many little craggy lines. Miguel's eyes followed their arc from Genoa to the Rhine — RHENUS FLUVIUS. A bearded man poured water from a jug, nearly covering the word BASILEA.

How easily attainable it seemed, across inch-wide hills and plains, this place where lived a man who had known his father and was holding the dead man's legacy in his custody!

Keeping Saragossa and Basel between his index and little fingers, he drew a circle with this improvised compass and found that Padua lay outside its circumference. The journey, though difficult, would be somewhat shorter than he had anticipated.

What about money? He would have to make do with the few escudos drawn on his otherwise impounded letter of credit. After all, he would not be the first Spaniard to make it over the mountains, although an escape from the clutches of the Holy Office would not be easy. There seemed to be no shelter against this madness save pure luck. Well, he would see to it that luck was on his side.

Again he pored over the map. Was there no better way

to go to Basel than across France, where any Spaniard, fugitive or not, could expect to run the gauntlet between Papists and Huguenots? Advice from Don Fernando? As one of the Emperor's captains, Montoya had crisscrossed the continent in many campaigns and knew its roads and bypaths. Miguel dismissed the thought at once. If he made good his escape, then Padre Domingo would be bound to question the old soldier and his wife. Ignorance would have to be their shield. But Paca? Well, he would have to lie to her, invent some voyage to Toledo with the padre, something that would prevent her from running over to the Montoyas and announcing his disappearance. Once he was gone for good, they would surely take her in.

He looked at the map. Perhaps he should try to get to Italy first and then make his way over the Alps. One mountain more or less . . . He laughed, excitement slowly rising in him. The candle was burning low. He started off to fetch another from the kitchen.

On the inner balcony he smelled the smoke from a coal basin coming up from the patio. There by the light of a lantern, in the cool of the night, Paca was pressing his shirts, lovingly guiding the iron into each and every ruffle.

redo," Padre Domingo intoned as he stood on the main altar of Saragossa's cathedral. He was surrounded by the lower clergy and by tapers that, with their golden light, vied with the jewel-like stained-glass windows in illuminating the somber nave.

"... *in unum Deum, Factorem coeli et terrae, visibilium et invisibilium*," answered the voices, filling the soaring vault.

It seemed to Miguel as if they were moving slowly, blissfully, each voice in its own orbit, yet encountering one another again and again in a soft and sudden glow. The mighty pillars seemed to give a measure to this dance. He marveled that he was seeing with his ears and hearing with his eyes. Was it in such moments of luminous beholding that men resolved to kill and die for what they called their Faith?

The voices fell silent. Padre Domingo began to recite the Collect. Miguel let his eyes roam along the nave's wall. There were side altars, their martyr-patrons depicted with the instruments of their wretched deaths — wheels, arrows, roasting spits. How wasted they were, he thought, those ecstatic, emaciated martyrs, as well as the thousands and thousands of less celebrated creatures dying at the stake, on the gallows, on the block, each one a miracle of the

Creator's craftsmanship whose workings were just beginning to be revealed to dazzled minds. Was there no end to those crude pictures?

At the end of the aisle, on a pedestal, there stood a life-size statue of the Virgin, sumptuously clad and crowned, a vapid smile painted on her glistening face. Miguel, however, did not look at her countenance. He stared at her necklace. It was his mother's.

He saw himself again, almost seven years old, thrilled and impatient. His parents were going to give a dinner party for a gentleman passing through Saragossa. He would be allowed to stay up late and greet the guest of honor. The latter turned out to be a dashing young man who had swung the boy into the air and called him his "godbrother." It was Don Juan, the Emperor's son. Miguel remembered his parents in festive dress, Juan quietly handsome, Marguerite radiant in black silk, the ruby necklace around her collar.

"Too bad about that ruff," she had said to Paca, who helped her fasten the clasp. "It takes away from the stones. When this piece was made for my grandmother, a woman was still allowed to show off her assets!"

There was a painting in the house in Ghent, he recalled, of Great-grandmother Steen coiffed by a kind of veil-draped sugar cone, the necklace displayed on her white shoulders.

And now it hung on that stupid doll.

A shudder ran down his spine. Men were sent to the stake for lesser blasphemies. From the corner of his eye he glanced at the people next to him. They seemed unconcerned. That stupid doll, he repeated to himself with savage satisfaction.

The voices were singing again, but their spell was broken,

74

or rather, Miguel did not allow himself to be enthralled again. He had to have his wits about him, for Communion was at hand. He had come to Mass to show himself to Padre Domingo. Having owned up to a couple of sins of the flesh to some half-deaf monk, he found that he was now in a reasonable state of grace.

"*Mea culpa*" — the padre beat his breast with a pudgy hand. Miguel advanced toward the high altar.

Padre Domingo looked surprised. He did not know what to make of young Roxas' presence. Miguel had not left the house since his return from Toledo — this much the padre knew. The stroll to the ramparts had not been reported to him for reasons of Camacho's own. Padre Domingo wished he could have Miguel watched a little more closely, but this would have been against his instructions. "Invisible," the cardinal had said.

The padre, along with the benefit of doubt, gave the young man the wafer. Miguel took care to swallow it whole. Not long ago a man had inadvertently bitten into the Host. They had pulled out all his teeth, and his tongue for good measure.

The padre read the postcommunion and, with a resounding "*Ite, missa est*," dismissed the congregation.

Miguel let himself be swept along by the crowd. At the portal he spotted the Montoyas. Don Fernando must have seen him, but he stared straight ahead. Doña Soledad accepted the young man's glance with eyes full of sorrow. Then she pulled her veil over her face.

San Isidro's Altare Pigrorum — the late Mass — had dismissed its faithful, Paca among them. She had just made it to the low Mass, which was read in the little church for the town's slugabeds, though she was anything but lazy, having been busy since early morning preparing Miguel's Sunday dinner. She had left the soup and the fried chicken in the hearth's hot embers and was now hurrying home to ready the meal and set the table. She was panting a little; her legs gave her trouble; and her black silk kerchief did nothing to protect her from the burning noon rays.

As she approached the house, she frowned. Who was that creature loitering near the entrance? There were altogether too many beggars around the square lately. She would have to give the man a coin and tell him to move on, to spy on someone else, she suddenly thought, with dull apprehension. It all began with that accursed day when Don Juan had let those Christ-killers into his wine cellar, and God knew what troubles lay still ahead.

Paca had no quarrel with the Jews; in fact, she had rarely encountered one. But she had been taught from childhood on to accept the Church's pronouncements without challenge by her otherwise hard and sharp common sense. She believed that the Jews murdered Christian children much the same way she knew that San Isidro's finger bone worked miracles.

She reached the gate. As she was about to insert the key into the lock, the man suddenly stood beside her.

"Good day, Cousin Paca," he said, pushing his slouch hat somewhat out of his face.

"Camacho!" She gasped. "You thief, you wretch! Where are our candlesticks; where is my rosary?"

"Gently, Cousin Paca. Don't work yourself into a fit. I have to talk to you."

"I'll have no truck with a thief. By the way, where is Doña Marguerita's egg?"

"Her egg. You've hit the nail on the head."

She eyed him suspiciously. The "egg," a so-called *Nürnberger Ei*, was one of the newfangled pocket watches invented in that German town and exported from there all over Europe. Marguerite had worn hers pomander-fashion, suspended from her belt, until the day it disappeared, together with Camacho. Had he not gambled it away long ago?

He took his time.

"Her egg," he finally repeated. "I mean her young one."

Paca felt her heartbeat falter. "Yes?" she whispered.

"He wants to bolt."

"How do you know?"

"Never mind. I know. And so do you."

"I know nothing. Let me in," she said, panting, trying to push him aside. He grabbed her wrist and twisted it expertly.

"You stay here, Cousin Paca, if you please, and listen to me. Your precious Miguel wants to make a run for it. The padre won't like that, but he doesn't want to lock him up. He has his reasons. So he has me watching him from afar."

"You . . . you . . ."

"Yes, Paca, I. To make it short: I cannot be after him day and night. So, if you miss him for more than three hours, you will let me know. The Church of Saint Tecla. If he slips through our fingers and I do not hear from you, I shall tell the padre that you helped him get away. Then you will hang; that is, if you are lucky. Good day, Cousin Paca."

He was gone.

"You scum!" She wanted to scream the words after him. They came out as a whisper. Fighting for breath, she leaned against the house wall.

So Miguel was thinking of flight. She had guessed it all along. What was she to do? If she kept quiet, she would disobey the Church, she who broke no fast, who never missed Mass. But by talking she would betray Miguel. How could she ever denounce him to that rot, that Camacho?

Her thoughts running in a mad circle, she felt her heart beating, its pulses echoing in her head. She sank down on the cobblestones, the sun, she fancied, blazing down on her from a pitch-black sky. Shafts of fire stabbed through her head. She fell into a bottomless pit.

Miguel, arriving from Mass, parted the gathering of curious souls — churchgoers and idlers — around Paca. They had carried her into the shade. Her face was flushed and swollen. He knelt beside her, pulled out his dagger, slit her sleeve, and located the vein. The blood oozed out lazily.

Paca was buried the following day in San Isidro's narrow churchyard. As they lowered the coffin into the hole and the first shovelful of sod fell on the dully resounding wood, it seemed to Miguel that they were burying the last of his childhood. There was sadness in the notion and an odd sense of deliverance.

The evening after Paca's burial Miguel washed and put on fresh clothes. In his black coat, black doublet, and black hose he did not look much different from any of the students flocking back to the university for fall term.

He ripped the page of Europe from the *Orbis Pictus*, folded it, and put it into his belt pouch, which already held thirty goldpieces — all of his travel money. Then he put the heavy book back on the shelf. Should he cut away his mother's portrait and take it along? No. The empty frame would indicate flight, but an untouched house might merely suggest a brief absence and thus delay pursuit.

He descended the wooden stairs, crossed the patio, passed through the entrance hall and through the front gate. He locked it and walked away without looking back.

There was much coming and going on the old bridge: townspeople taking the air, students strolling in groups. Miguel fell in with them and passed through the gate. He walked as if on wings. How easy it had been. He was now about three miles from town, keeping straight northward. That, too, was easy: the Big Dipper stood sparkling on the night sky. A better guide than Camacho, he thought, when, as if conjured up, the same Camacho stood before him. He held a knife in his hand. The moonlight played on the blade, whose tip looked strangely dull.

Miguel, about to draw his dagger, suddenly froze. Instinct warned him not to risk a knife fight with Camacho. "Why, it's you, Don Miguel," the latter said with mild reproach. "Too bad you did not engage my services beforehand. Now I shall have to double my fee."

"The little side income, right?" Miguel managed to say, playing for time.

"Precisely. And since it's you, Don Miguel, I shall content myself with twenty-five escudos. Otherwise I would be regrettably forced to alert a few soldiers on horseback."

Miguel surrendered the goldpieces.

"Many thanks, Don Miguel. And now let me give your money's worth."

Camacho had decided to satisfy himself with the ransom and to entrust Miguel to the hazards of a flight over the

79

mountains. It would not do to have him back alive to tell the padre about a certain private enterprise that for years had been poaching the Inquisition's grounds.

"Here, the river will guide you easily. About ten miles north you will come to a lake on your right. From there you have about fifty miles to Jaca. Near the town gate there is a hostelry, where you can rest. It's nothing fancy, but you will have a roof over your head. So will Don Gil, if he waits awhile. He might yet get yours. His own is too small for him and his growing family."

They walked a few steps, side by side. From the corner of his eye Miguel watched Camacho. What if the wretch changed his mind — went back to town and sent the guards after him? He might fear the padre more than Gil de Vega. Who could see through this murky soul? But how to get rid of him? The jugular? No. The pain would only madden him. The groin? Awkward from the side. The carotid? Definitely. One blow should fell him. It would also damage the windpipe. Let it be the carotid.

They kept walking. Between the poplar trees the river was shimmering.

"Here is the footpath, Don Miguel," Camacho said, "and if you follow the Galle——" With a gulping sound, he collapsed. Miguel, using the edge of his hand, had struck him on his bobbing Adam's apple. Dropping on his knee beside him, he delivered yet another blow against Camacho's head. Then he emptied the belt pouch, lifted the man, and threw him over his shoulder. Young and vigorous, Miguel should have carried him with ease, but the body seemed unduly heavy; its touch sickened him. At last, with a sigh of relief, he threw Camacho into the grass, dragged him to the edge of the water, and pushed him into the current. "Follow the Gallego!"

He found the trail again. How easy it was to walk at night! Trees and rocks became gliding shadows. The moon had set, but there was enough starlight to show him the mule trail. The cicadas fiddled. Saragossa, lying behind him, his father, his house, the cardinal, even the padre, who would send his men after him in a few days — everything had faded. There was only the bliss of striding ahead, of hurrying toward a goal.

Time flowed by, unmeasured, until the sky began to pale in the East. The night's spell was breaking. It was cold. Miguel wrapped himself in his coat, huddled under a tree, and surrendered to a sudden, leaden drowsiness.

The sun stood high when he awoke. Aching all over, he scrambled to his feet. He skidded down the stony riverbank, knelt by the current, and drank out of his hollowed hand to deceive his hunger. Then he climbed back to the trail.

Where were last night's seven-league boots? He plodded ahead, hot and sore. The sun was burning through his black doublet and casting a short shadow before him. After a while he stopped. This would not do. Any pursuer could spot him immediately, trudging along in his black garb on the gray-white, sun-glimmering path.

Rest, he told himself. Think. Make a plan. He looked for a place in the shade, nearly sat down, but jumped back, laughing and disbelieving. Sheep manure! He *was* tired. Why, then, there was only one thing to do: wait.

The grinding of wooden wheels on the scree did not surprise him. When he spied a mule, hitched to a cart with an old peasant sitting on its crossboard, Miguel smiled. It was as if he had coaxed them into appearing by his fervent wish.

"Go with God, señor," the old man greeted him.

"I would like to," Miguel answered.

The other one looked at him. "They are after you, señor?"

"Not yet."

Miguel did not have to explain his needs. The old man turned his creaking vehicle around. "Will you wait here, señor?"

Within half an hour he was back with the necessary items. Miguel, in the cool shadow of an oak tree, took off his doublet and shirt. Then he opened the sack the old man had handed him. Out came a shepherd's shirt. Miguel held his breath as he pulled it over his head. Coarse, dirty, and sweat-stiffened, it made his skin crawl. No matter. Off with the breeches and hose, the proud, spurred boots. On with the reeking pants, the leggings, the rope-soled canvas shoes. Under the shirt he put on his belt with the little moneybag. Then he reappeared at the cart. A goldpiece was offered and proudly refused. Miguel climbed on the crossboard, and the old man cracked his whip. Two peasants, munching sheep cheese and oil-roasted bread crumbs, were on their way to the fair at Ayerbe.

As the mule slowly dragged the cart uphill, Miguel tried to find his bearings. Things had happened too fast. Within the last twenty-four hours he had left his home, never to return, had become a fugitive, and had killed his first man.

They were approaching Ayerbe. Miguel shook his head to clear it. He could not allow himself to follow the direction his thoughts were taking, for he would need all his energy to outwit his pursuers, who were probably already on their way.

Don Fernando de Montoya and his wife were having dinner when a terrified servant announced the visit of Padre Domingo.

The monk entered the dining room. Montoya rose, and so did Doña Soledad.

"What brings me this honor, Reverend Father?"

He did not offer the padre a seat.

"An accident, Your Grace, that needs explanation. One of the Office's servants has been missing for several days. Yesterday his body was washed ashore under the bridge. He had drowned."

Montoya made no reply.

"My servant Camacho was instructed to watch Miguel de Roxas, who disappeared more than a week ago. I have reason to believe that this young man may have had a hand in my servant's death."

"How? Your Reverence just stated that Camacho drowned. Were there signs of violence on the body?"

"None. This corroborates my suspicion. Roxas is a student of medicine. He knows where to strike. Also, the body had obviously been in the water for days, yet it was found near the bridge. It must have been swept along by the Gallego. Roxas probably has taken the path northward. You would oblige me by telling me when he left."

"I have not spoken to Miguel de Roxas since the day he alighted from your carriage, Reverend Father. And I have not seen him since last Sunday's mass."

Padre Domingo listened not so much to Montoya's words

as to the sound of his voice. It had the ease of truth. There was none of the halting rigidity the Dominican's experienced ear often detected when interrogating suspects.

"What about his horse?"

"It is still stabled with my mounts. He has not claimed it."

The padre reflected. Should he subject Montoya to the Question? Probably not. The tough old soldier would let them break his every bone without batting an eyelid. Besides, it looked as if, indeed, he knew nothing of the matter. What about the wife?

For a few endless seconds his eyes gauged the composure of Doña Soledad. She was standing still and bolt upright. Fernando de Montoya felt for his dagger. His wife would not have to face the rack.

The wave rose, crested, and subsided. The padre took his leave.

Doña Soledad had not moved. Now she swayed a little. Her husband put his arm around her shoulder, led her to an easy chair, and made her sit down. Then he left the dining room and went down into the wine cellar. In the corner there stood a barrel of Burgundy, vintage 1555, a gift from the Emperor. Montoya called no servant. He pulled the tap, brought a bottle upstairs to Doña Soledad, and filled the crystal goblets.

The wine glowed like rubies as the two silently raised their glasses.

In Ayerbe, Miguel took leave of his taciturn companion. Spending five of his thirty escudos, he bought a mule, a loaf of bread, some cheese, and a leather flask, which he filled with spring water. Then he set out again on the narrow mountain trail, which now ran up the steep side of the ever-narrowing Gallego Gorge.

It would take the padre between three days and a week, he figured, to be aware of his flight. With luck, he could reach the frontier in three days. The mule, however, was in no hurry and was unimpressed by the heel kicks of its rider's canvas shoes.

On the second day Miguel heard hoofbeats behind him. He pulled the dirty kerchief over his forehead and made himself hang sleepily in the saddle. Riding single file, a troop of soldiers overtook him one by one.

"How far to Jaca?" their leader called out to him.

" 'Bout forty miles, señor," Miguel answered in his thickest dialect. It would not have fooled a mountain-dweller, but Captain Guzmán's Castilian ears were not fine-tuned to the regional shades of Aragonese speech. The soldiers rode on.

Miguel fell back and waited. As soon as the dust had settled, he left the main track and took one of the steep, overgrown paths leading up the wooded ridge. Soon the trail was lost in the underbrush. When he could not bring his stubborn mount to advance farther through thorns and brambles, he alighted, took off the saddle, and threw it into the bushes. The useless beast would have to fend for itself.

He shouldered the sack with his clothes and food and began climbing straight up, hauling himself from tree to tree, often skidding on the needle-covered slope. At last he reached the crest of the ridge, only to look down into a narrow gorge, with the next hillock looming beyond. The sun was already low, its slanting, golden shafts glowing between the fir trees. Miguel crossed the long shadows, parting ferns and brush, fighting his way through honey-suckle and whitethorn. Straight north!

As he slid down a boulder, he saw the sprawling root of an oak tree offering a hold. He grabbed at it. When he heard the hiss, it was too late. There was a sliver of pain in his hand and a flash of black and yellow lightning in the grass. He looked at his palm. Two tiny fang marks showed on it, right under the thumb. He was not frightened, but felt a strange light-headedness, almost an urge to laugh. Was this to be the end of his journey? Death in this God-forsaken spot? Not as long as there was breath in him, he vowed, suddenly sober again. He made a tourniquet from his kerchief and began to suck the wound. But why did the blood keep hammering in his temples? And what about those shapes? Why was his mother talking to Padre Domingo?

His left hand clamped to the piece of cloth around his right wrist, he fainted.

Captain Guzmán and his men rode into Jaca. He quartered them among the frightened townspeople and went immediately to see the bishop.

The latter was a tight-fisted Aragonese who resented the demands on his parishioners' meager resources and, even more, the infringement on the old privileges of the Kingdom of Aragón. No outsider (such as the Castilian Guzmán) was to impose his law on Aragonese burghers. The bishop, with the tough common sense of the miser, also detested the indiscriminate persecution of converts. Why kill off tradesmen whose work was good and cheap? Besides, the Church had made a bargain with them. Renounce your false gods, she had said, and you shall live. Such going back on a deal offended the bishop's sense of justice.

He looked with ill-concealed contempt at Captain Guzmán, who had just asked for rigorous interrogation of the townspeople.

"Juan de Roxas' son, right? It seems to me that his father was apprehended without regard of his privileges. Miguel de Roxas would be granted asylum here."

Captain Guzmán almost choked. He knew Aragonese insubordination, although the presence of the Holy Office was holding it down in Saragossa. It was different with these mountain folk. (He would report on the bishop to Padre Domingo.)

"Your Grace will at least permit an announcement with drums — to declare Roxas' flight and the prize on his head."

"Drum away, my son," the bishop replied pleasantly. "Drum all you want."

Fray Antón, brother apothecary at the monastery of San Juan de la Peña, was gathering juniper berries to distill them into the convent's famous cordial. Picking his way through the brambles, he nearly overlooked the whitish bundle lying crumpled under a boulder. As he bent over it, he saw the ashen face and the right arm, which was swollen to double size. The left hand, slender and long-fingered — not a peasant's hand, the brother noticed — still held the tourniquet. Fray Antón lost no time. He put down his pail, lifted the limp body from the ground, and carried it the two miles to the convent.

The brother surgeon was summoned; a cell was readied.

After two days of delirium and a few more of convalescence, Miguel rallied, thanks partly to his youth and partly to the elixirs of the good monks.

Meanwhile, the brother steward, returning with supplies from Jaca, brought the news that one Miguel de Roxas, fugitive from the authority of the Holy Office and son of the late Juan de Roxas (who had been condemned to death for criminally conniving with Jews), was, if possible, to be apprehended and delivered alive into the hands of Captain Guillermo de Guzmán, emissary of the Holy Office at Saragossa. The prize on Roxas' head was a hundred escudos.

As Miguel lay on his bed, this was announced with drums to a sullen crowd in the marketplace.

The prior entered the guest cell. Miguel was asleep. The desperate will in the young face had dissolved; it was trust that the old man read in the uncontrolled features.

Criminally conniving with Jews — or had this been the accusation against the young man's father? The prior did not care to split hairs. His mother had been a Jewish Conversa, and he had taken refuge in the very Church that had forced her to renounce the God of her fathers.

He woke Miguel and pointed to the sack in the corner that Fray Antón had fetched when he went back for his berry pail. "Get dressed," he said, "and remember to wear the clothes you were found in — no doublet and spurs."

They both smiled.

The prior led the way, and they passed through the cloister. Its garden, sheltered from the wind and tended by the monks, was flowering, although outside the leaves were wilting and falling. Miguel felt that he had been similarly protected and was now to brave the autumn storms.

Leaving the monastery, they arrived at a meadow near the rim of the woods. From his cloak, the prior pulled out a whistle and blew it. It made a shrill sound.

Within moments, a shape, half child, half monster, appeared from the forest. Its huge head sat on a neck with a goiter; its eyes protruded. Yet it moved nimbly on its ungainly legs. Such misbegotten beings were not infrequently seen in the mountains; Miguel had read about them in his anatomy textbooks, but he had never beheld one. At other times his scientific curiosity would have been stirred by such an opportunity; he would have studied the creature from all sides and observed its living habits. Now, he merely welcomed the apparition as yet another aide on his dangerous journey.

These *bozales* — as they were called in the Pyrenees — were used by the peasants for the lowest menial tasks. The prior, apparently, had won the trust and devotion of this particular one. He was now talking to the creature in curious signs and guttural sounds.

"He will lead you over the mountain," he then said to Miguel, who kissed the prior's hand and wanted to thank him. The monk shook his head and gave him his blessing: "Go with God, my son."

He followed his strange guide. The monster, carrying Miguel's sack, climbed like a mountain goat. After long hours of crawling and hoisting they reached a wind-blown crest. Miguel saw the Pyrenees' range, spreading from west to east, its heights emerging from a sea of clouds. He had to hold on to his companion before he dared to look down the precipice, over the tree tops into the long, narrow valley, where at the bottom he could make out a toylike church tower surrounded by minute stone huts.

The *bozal* began the descent ahead of Miguel, holding and supporting him on the treacherous schist. At last they reached the timberline. The forest creature handed Miguel his bundle and climbed back, crawling upward as quickly as a bug on a stone. It disappeared.

Miguel had to lean against a tree, overcome by weakness. He was free, he said to himself. Free. Yet his eyes were still watchful, his head quick to turn. The weight of fear was lifted, but his soul was still bending under it when suddenly such joy shot up from his heart that it was almost too much to bear. He embraced the tree and kissed the rough bark. Then he climbed down into the valley, toward the first village in the Kingdom of France.

Captain Guzmán had his men fan out from the headquarters at Jaca and watch the mountain passes at Canfranc, at Panticosa, and even at Urgel.

After three weeks he had to admit that he was beaten.

Back in Saragossa Padre Domingo was no luckier than his subordinates. Finally he had to go to Toledo and confess to Don Pedro that Miguel had escaped.

There was a faraway look in the cardinal's eyes. He kept silent for a while. Then he said: "It does not matter. Someday he will return to Padua. When this comes to pass, I wish to be apprised of it."

ART 2

t was on the afternoon before Candlemas that Miguel rode into Basel. He rode, having bought a horse with the money he had made in France.

On leaving Montpellier he had had the choice between acquiring a warm coat and buying a mount. Under the Provence's gentle sky the choice had not been difficult. But as he was riding toward Avignon, the Mistral blew through his shirt and doublet and thin coat, making him consider selling his horse and continuing on foot, warmly clothed. It was a toss between chilblains and blisters, and in the end he had opted to keep the horse. He regretted it now, for the slanting rays of the winter sun, while setting all the town's bull's-eye windows on fire, did nothing to keep him from shivering with cold. He would have to get a thicker coat. But with what money? The question did not unduly worry him.

How had it been in Spain? There, you were born rich or poor (mostly poor), the way you were born straight or crooked. As he never would have dreamed of telling a hunchback to stand erect, so it would never have occurred to him to tell a beggar to work for a living. Whenever he happened to have no money on him and a wretch would extend a bony hand, Miguel would say, "Forgive me, brother, for the sake of Our Lord," as any Spaniard would.

93

He had now exactly three florins to his name. But he did not belong to the brotherhood of the poor, however empty his pockets. Poverty was a disease, chronic, incurable, God-ordained. Being short of money was merely a problem to be solved. Had he not solved it many times since he had set out from Saragossa with thirty escudos in his belt pouch?

He spurred his horse and soon halted in front of the Hedgehog, a hostelry some vagrant scholar had recommended as the cheapest hole available.

Cheap or not, the Hedgehog's taproom boasted a stout tile stove with a wooden bench running around it.

After stabling his horse, Miguel entered and sank on this bench, legs outstretched, his back caressed by the warmth of the glazed bosses. After a while, though, he felt hungry, and soon was sitting over a cheese soup so thick that the spoon stood up in it.

His table companion, also a wandering scholar to judge from his clothes and his easy Latin, asked Miguel where he came from.

"France," Miguel answered, spooning his soup.

"Indeed! That's a mischievous land, comrade."

Miguel nodded noncommittally. He did not share that opinion. Avoiding a dispute, he let the other one complain about French stinginess, French lechery, French dirt, and followed his own thoughts.

He had fared well in France.

There had been the priest in that first Pyrenean village who had taken him in, cold and exhausted, and had made him rest a few days before sending him on his journey with good advice and a basket of food. He had shown him the way on the wrinkled map from the *Orbis Pictus*.

"Go toward the Garonne, son," he had said. "They are having the grape harvest now and can use any and every pair of hands — or feet. It will help you along."

At first he had stared uncomprehendingly at his host. He — harvesting grapes? He had hoped for a recommendation to the University of Toulouse or of Montpellier, maybe to do some clerking — but peasant work . . .?

He would never forget the look of scorn in the eyes of the old man, who had guessed his indignation.

"So?" the priest had said. "Jesus was a carpenter's son; He certainly had to help in the shop. Peter was a fisherman. That's what is wrong with you Spaniards, your foolish, hollow conceit. True, you can still turn to highway robbery. That would suit a — how do you call yourself, a *hidalgo*? — much better. But then you would sooner or later decorate the gallows down in Toulouse . . ."

Ashamed, Miguel had dutifully kissed the irate reverend's hand and gone on his way. He had found the harvesters trampling grapes, which, surprisingly, was a pleasure, for it cooled the blisters on his feet, and hoisting baskets, which was a chore. But afterward he would sit down to eat with the laborers, sharing their good food as he had shared their toil.

The grape season over, he had worked on a farm, cutting wood and building a fence. Then there had been Marion, widow and châtelaine, who had held him prisoner of her soft arms for two weeks until the night he had climbed down from her bedroom window and continued his journey.

And Montpellier! A scholar in Toulouse had given him a recommendation to Professor Grenier, anatomist at the university there. Grenier had turned out to be a fat, hot-tempered man who had welcomed Miguel as a long-awaited rescuer.

"A Paduan! Just what I need!" And he had led him into a cellar that was filled with human bones heaped together every which way.

"I need these threaded and mounted," Grenier had declared. "You can get at least half a dozen skeletons out of them. My students are all bunglers, but you will do splendidly." Then he had pointed to a crudely carpented table on which wire, needles, scissors, saws, and tweezers were strewn about, together with a dog-eared copy of the *Fabrica* open at the page on the mounting of skeletons.

"I shall pay you twelve florins apiece," Grenier had added, and left the premises.

It was an ungrateful task; most of the bones were brittle and unthreadable. Miguel, after toiling for two weeks in the anatomist's untidy cellar, had finally come up with two skeletons and a dwarf from the leftovers.

There followed a quarrel with Grenier, who had refused to pay the twelve florins apiece, complaining that the specimens were knock-kneed and crookedly assembled and that one of them was holding a broom instead of the scythe or trident suggested in the *Fabrica*. In the end, Miguel had drawn his dagger and threatened to kill the professor in order to have fresh, threadable bones to construct a skeleton to the latter's satisfaction. Grenier had finally consented to pay twelve florins for each of the full-size specimens but only six for the dwarf.

For sixteen florins Miguel had bought the horse, which, walking slowly and resting often, carried him from Montpellier to Basel. He had made some money here and there, setting bones and stitching together a few wounds. In an Avignon hostelry he even had had the opportunity to save a guest's life by preventing him from choking on a chicken bone. Rescued, the man had rewarded him with three gold-pieces that had lasted the rest of the journey.

Instinctively, Miguel looked around — but no one was strangling on cheese soup. His table companion had fallen silent.

He rose and went over to the host to negotiate a bed for the night.

Old Babeli, housekeeper to Master Bartholomaeus Faber, shuffled through the oak-paneled corridor in answer to the door knocker.

The young man outside did not look too prosperous. He wore a thin coat over his doublet that had seen better days. A poor student, probably, looking for a handout. Master Barthel seemed to attract them the way honey did flies. Yet the visitor reminded her of somebody, a young version of an older face, not too much older, though . . .

"What do you want?" she asked. "Today is Sunday. The master has gone to church."

Miguel tried to grasp the sense of the gruff greeting, proffered in an impenetrable Basler dialect. "Master Bartholomaeus Faber?" he pronounced as distinctly as he could.

"I told you, gone to church," Babeli yelled, as if raising her voice would make the foreigner understand her language. She pointed to the tower of Saint Catherine. The bells were ringing.

"Mass!" Babeli cried. "Come tomorrow. Monday. Today — *Sunday*. You — *Monday*."

97

Miguel understood and withdrew. On his way back to the Hedgehog, he had already crossed the narrow alley by the church when he heard a man call out, "Greetings, Master Faber and Miss Vrone!"

He looked around and saw a pair coming down the lane. There was a gray-haired gentleman, wrapped in a coat of marten, his fine features showing displeasure as he threaded his way between puddles of snow water. With him was a girl, about eighteen or nineteen, dressed in black velvet. Two heavy, dark blond braids fell down her back. She was carrying a missal.

Monsieur Brantôme, the century's arbiter on feminine beauty, would not have given her a second look. She was too slender for the day's taste, almost thin. Her nose and chin were definitely too pointed (a sign of money-mindedness), but they were set off by a pair of gray eyes, luminous, although a little near-sighted, and a mouth that was fresh, finely chiseled, and quick to laugh.

For the most part keeping by the side of the elderly man, she occasionally would jump over a puddle, then with a smile of good-natured impatience wait for her slow-walking companion.

Miguel followed them with his eyes until they rounded the corner. Then he returned to his quarters and spent the rest of the day with his new found friend, the tile stove.

On Monday morning he presented himself again at Faber's house, this time handing Babeli a piece of paper with his name written on it. Within moments, Faber hurried to the door. "Miguel de Roxas! Come in, come in!" The Latin was pronounced with easy precision.

Once they were in the drawing room, the printer's eyes traveled over the young man's threadbare clothes. Something was wrong. Surely the older Roxas had enough money to have his son properly outfitted for a journey.

"Miguel," he said, "above all: How is your father? I have not heard from him for months. Is he well?"

"Thank you, Master Faber, quite well."

Bartholomaeus gave a sigh of relief. "Thank God! I feared something might have happened to him."

"I said he was well, Master Faber. I did not say he was alive."

Bartholomaeus Faber stood still, the color quickly vanishing from his face. He indicated a chair and sat down in another. "Tell me what happened."

Miguel had finished.

Faber rose. "I am glad that you have come," he said simply.

"I shall go on to Padua," Miguel hastened to say, eager to forestall any other questions the printer might have. But Faber seemed in no hurry to discuss the young man's plans. "First," he said, "let us have something to eat. And then we might stroll over to the shop and see about the manuscript."

Bartholomaeus had had a hearty lunch, but he judged that his young visitor could do with some food. He had Babeli set the table again and went through the motions of nibbling on a piece of roast chicken while Miguel cleaned his plate with thoroughness, wondering why Faber's daughter did not share their meal.

The printshop, a low building with a red roof, was situated in the same narrow street, about twenty paces from the house. There were five long, vaulted halls. One contained the huge press; the next was full of drying racks for the freshly printed sheets; the third housed the bindery; the fourth was the composition room; and the fifth was a library that doubled as an office, with a large working table and several stools in its middle. Daylight fell through the deep-silled windows. Their bull's-eye glass panels were transparent.

"My idea," Faber said. "Why shut out the daylight?"

But Miguel had not heard. Speechless, he was staring at the girl who was advancing toward him, the one he had seen the day before. She now wore a blue twill skirt and bodice, covered by a drab-colored apron. Her hair was wound in a top-knot. Several black smudges adorned her face. On her nose sat a pair of iron-rimmed spectacles, and in her left hand she was holding a wrench.

"Miguel de Roxas, student at Padua" — Faber presented the young man to her — "my daughter, Veronica."

The girl wiped her slender, ink-smeared hand on her apron and offered it to Miguel. "Welcome to Basel, scholar from Padua," she greeted him in the choicest Latin.

"You . . . you speak . . ."

"Nothing to it." She laughed. "Besides, it's part of the business."

"Veronica runs the firm," Faber thought necessary to explain.

"So I gather," Miguel answered, trying to regain his composure.

The girl now addressed her father in their native tongue, her clear soprano plunging back into her throat, from where it came forth again through a barrier of hissing and rasping consonants. She seemed amused.

Faber reverted to Latin. "Miguel would like to see his father's Vita," he said.

The girl drew in her breath a little. "The Roxas manuscript? They're working on it right now," she said apologetically. "Could you wait for about three days?"

"Why, certainly," said Miguel.

"Where are you staying?"

"At the Hedgehog."

"Dear me!" she exclaimed.

"I believe we can do better than that," Faber interjected.

"Of course, Father. I'll tell Babeli to have the guest room ready."

She turned again to Miguel before he was able to thank her. "You're studying at Padua? Then you must have some usable Italian, yes?"

He nodded.

"So much the better," she declared in a Tuscan as flawless as her Latin. "That's a more comfortable house-language."

While she was talking, a dignified black tomcat made its entrance into the workroom. It walked right over to Miguel and rubbed its head against his boots.

"That's Lucifer," Vrone said. "He works in the paper stacks. He keeps the mice out. But now you must excuse me" — she waved the wrench — "those bunglers have bent one of the press's bolts. I have to see what I can do. Till supper!"

She ran off, the cat following her with deliberate, silky tread.

Miguel, by now thoroughly unsettled, slowly put his hand against his forehead. Faber laughed.

"She has the best business head on her shoulders I have

101

ever seen," he said. "I have no sons. So why not give her a chance?"

"But her Latin . . . her Italian . . ."

"I taught her. At first it was a game, but she soaked it up like a sponge. So we began to study in earnest. You should hear her Greek," Faber added with a sort of embarrassed pride. "But now let me show you a little of what we are doing."

They looked at some woodblocks and at the layout for several books, among them a superb new edition of Cicero's *Disputationes Tusculanae*, which Faber had annotated.

As the short afternoon turned into darkness, the workers stopped at the press.

"We do not do anything by candlelight," Faber explained. "There is altogether too much paper around here. We don't want to burn the place down. So we get up with the chickens and close shop with them."

The dinner table reunited the three.

Vrone had changed into a black dress with white collar and had braided her hair. The ink smears on her face and hands had disappeared. She looked somewhat solemn. There evidently had been a conference between father and daughter, and its result was to be announced at dessert.

"Miguel," Faber began, "I assume you will go back to the Hedgehog to fetch your stuff. What about your horse?"

"I think I can have it stabled there for a few days, Master Faber."

"So you are set to go to Padua as soon as you have seen your father's manuscript?"

"Yes, Master Faber."

"What about your tuition money?"

"I don't know yet. But I have a colleague there, a friend, Vitus Trachter. He gets by with a pittance, clerking for the law professors. I could do that too."

Faber looked at him sharply. "I believe you," he said. "I am certain you could make it through that grind. But I have another proposition for you: How would you like to work for us as a corrector? My eyes are giving out, and good ones are few and far between. You could earn your tuition in six months, and at the next vacation you would be welcome to make some money here again; that is, if some prince has not snatched you away in the meantime to be his physician."

Miguel looked at Vrone, who had bitten into an apple and was now swallowing quickly, seeming to feel more keenly than the young man himself that a word from her would tip the scale of his decision.

"Bring your horse," she said. "Ours doesn't want to pull the sleigh anymore."

"Mine wouldn't either." He laughed. Then, serious, he turned to the old printer. "Master Faber," he said, "I shall be happy to work for you."

"Good. You can have one of the apprentice's rooms. It's under the eaves, but you have young legs, and the view from there is not at all bad."

Miguel plunged into his new endeavor eagerly; he had had too long a vacation from mental discipline. He worked well with Vrone, admiring her sharp, rational mind, which at once separated in everything the essential from the non-essential. Yet had anyone suggested that he was attracted to her, he would have found the idea outlandish indeed. More sprite than woman, entirely unlike Angiolina and the other Paduan beauties, whose obvious charms assaulted the senses, Vrone amused and challenged him, but she hardly stirred his desire.

Besides, he was going back to Padua in six months.

Meanwhile, without being fully aware of it, he was happy. It was exhilarating to be expected to do outstanding work. How pleasant to be busy, to be in a hurry! He had almost forgotten the purpose of his coming to Basel. His father's manuscript had by now been out of the composition room for more than two weeks, but he had not asked Vrone for it. He procrastinated.

Vrone, meanwhile, was waiting for him to mention the Vita, but she hesitated to press him, for she guessed that he was bracing himself for the task. She thought of him, sitting in his chamber, reading his father's last writings by the light of a trembling candle flame, fingering the pages on which Juan de Roxas' hands had lain.

Maybe it would be easier for him to do it in daylight and with someone else?

She did not reflect long.

The next morning she entered the workroom, Juan de Roxas' manuscript in one hand, a bunch of galley sheets in the other. "Miguel," she said, "your father's Vita is ready. I need you for proofreading."

He looked up from his Cicero, disturbed and grateful at the same time. She handed him the pages covered with his father's neat-flowing script and sat down at the table with the proofs.

"Juan de Roxas, Vita," she began. "Sheet One."

And Miguel felt the clear voice exorcizing the shadows.

THE AUTHOR TO BARTHOLOMAEUS FABER, PRINTER AND BOOK-
SELLER IN BASEL:

My dear Friend:

*It was with surprise and pleasure that I received your
letter asking me for an account of my life, to be included
in your* SPECULUM SCIENTIAE, *a collection of biographies of
our day's physicians and naturalists.*

*You thus want me to take my place among the Cardani,
Fallopii, Vesalii. Yet I was no more than their diligent
pupil who, unlike them, has not contributed anything to
our knowledge of the Creator's most astonishing work —
the human body. All I succeeded in doing was mitigating
pain and, sometimes, healing.*

*In another respect, however, I deem it worthwhile to set
down my recollection of things past.*

*I came into the world early in a century brimful with
great possibilities. It was good to be alive then. Did we
not witness the flowering of the new knowledge? Did
we not have a powerful Emperor, sponsor and protector
of the young sciences? A new Golden Age had announced
itself.*

It was not to be.

*Now that the old evils have returned tenfold and our
hopes are blighted, it pleases me to return to those years
when splendid things were possible.*

Receive then, dear friend, these scattered memoirs, and take from them whatever you deem useful to your enterprise.

With my heartfelt good wishes,
    Juan de Roxas
    June 15, A.D. 1580

I WAS BORN AT SARAGOSSA ON JULY 1, 1520, TO FRANCISCO DE ROXAS AND HIS WIFE, ISABEL DE LANUZA.

The Roxases were an old family, sufficiently noble, but they had fallen on bad days. At the time of my birth my parents owned not much more than their run-down town house and a few olive trees in the Gallego Valley.

Life was quiet in Saragossa, except for those few adventurers who would find their way to Palos to climb aboard a ship sailing for New Spain, whence they hoped to return with sacks of gold. (We never saw any of them again.)

After I learned my trivium at the monastery school, my father pondered my future. In his mind, there were three careers open to me, according to the adage of "Sea, Church, or Court." I showed no inclination to sail the Mediterranean (and to land on the rowing bench of a Turkish galley), nor did I want to become a priest. There remained only a position at court. My father saw me as a councillor or minister to our glorious Emperor Charles. Therefore, straining his scant resources to the utmost, he sent me to Salamanca to study the law and, in this way, to prepare myself for my lofty career.

Unfortunately, it turned out that I had little liking for tortuous legal treatises. I felt uneasy squandering my father's precious few maravedis on the pursuit of studies that annoyed and bored me, and would quickly have left Salamanca had I not thought of his disappointment at seeing me come home without a degree in the law, which to his mind would have facilitated my ascent at court.

One morning, as I walked along the river composing an explanatory letter to my father, I encountered a colleague who told me, greatly excited, that he was on his way to the "Anatomy," which was held yearly at the university. He invited me to accompany him. Out of idleness, and also because I wanted to postpone the unpleasant task of writing home, I acquiesced.

A classroom had been readied for the demonstration. On a wooden table there lay the corpse of one hanged that morning. I counted about two hundred spectators waiting for the professor. He came and sat down on his high cathedra while two barber-surgeons stood by with their knives at the ready.

The professor began reading from a book, which I learned afterward was Galen's De Ossibus, *while one of the barbers made an incision in the body from the tip of the pectoral bone to the umbilicus. A few of the spectators felt faint and withdrew into a corner, which allowed me to draw nearer.*

I marveled as the barbers laid open the ribs. I saw the lungs, wondrously protected by their bony cage, the stomach, so judiciously placed over the diaphragm. True, I had chanced on cut-open human bodies before this, the Lady Justice being wont to do her work in the market-place, but never had I looked at one as at a marvel of the Creator's handiwork.

The barbers denuded the right arm of its skin and the fascia. The muscles appeared. The two men worked away.

Suddenly, their knives touched each other for a moment and, amazing to behold, the cadaver's biceps contracted, making the forearm suddenly rise. We did not believe our eyes. The barbers made their blades touch again, and for the second time the dead limb flew up. I do not know to this day what caused the phenomenon — some metallic influence, perhaps — but I still remember my astonishment at the muscle that, by thickening, pulled up the forearm. The professor was droning on, but I did not hear him, exultant as I was, for I then knew that I would study medicine.

I dutifully finished the term, returned home, and broached the subject to my father.

The poor man lifted his hands in dismay.

"Medicine!" he exclaimed. "What an unheard-of thing for a Roxas! A proper Jew's calling!"

I remained steadfast. Fortunately, a friend of my father's knew Master Daza Chacón, one of the Emperor's physicians. He traveled to Madrid — a strenuous undertaking — to talk with the doctor. Only after Chacón had assured him that the art of healing was a noble endeavor indeed and that for instance Master Cornelius van Baersdorp, a prominent member of the Imperial medical staff, was of ancient Flemish lineage, did he give in.

In the fall of 1541 I was allowed to matriculate as a medical student at the University of Salamanca.

I threw myself into my work. Gone was the tedium of the law canons. I devoured the works of Hippocrates and Galen; of the latter I still know large parts by heart, useless though they are nowadays. I also wanted to read Rhazes and Maimonides. All the more as at the time there still was a chair of Arabic — and also one of Hebrew — at Salamanca.

Unfortunately, I could not readily follow the lectures there, having had no previous notion of those two difficult tongues. Thus I looked for a tutor among the many old Marranos who still lived in the quarter around the university. I found a certain Cide Gomez who, for a few maravedis a week, was willing to impart to me whatever knowledge he had of Arabic and Hebrew grammar and syntax. After the first few sessions, however, it became clear to me that this knowledge was limited to a few rudimentary rules that I could just as easily have learned by myself.

I told him that I had no intention of wasting my money; indeed, I wanted it back to give it to a better teacher. He let me vent my indignation for a while, then said that if I let him keep his fee, he would show me the path to the greatest scholar that ever trod the stones of Salamanca. I agreed, though still angry and none too confident, and he led me to a two-story house in a side lane. It had no balcony and only one grilled window on its narrow front. There, Gomez said, lived Eleazar Halevy, to whom not one of the university's learned men could be compared in knowledge of philosophy and of the ancient languages.

He knocked three times. After he had named himself, the door was opened by a boy of about fifteen years. There was a quick exchange in Arabic, of which I understood nothing, and the lad preceded us into a room that was dark until he hung up a copper oil lamp. By its light I beheld a chamber filled with books and scrolls. They were stacked on shelves along the walls and even strewn on the thick carpet. Never had I seen so many of them heaped together in such a small place. I had to think of my father's library, assembled on a few worm-eaten boards: the Old and New Testaments, the Missal, the Vita Sanctorum, Amadis de Gaula, *and, oddly enough, a few volumes of poetry. This room, however, could have been likened to a treasure cave from a tale of yore; one did not know where to begin. A copy of the Aldine* Iliad *lay open on the table. As I was leafing through it, the door opened and there entered a wizened hunchback clad in black robes, a black skullcap on his sparse white hair.*

He greeted me with friendliness. Apprised by Gomez, as it appeared, of my name and ambition, he told me that he would be glad to guide my studies. Anticipating my somewhat anxious inquiry about his fee, he assured me that he had no need of money, that learning brought its own reward. He would ask for no more than I had paid Gomez and only because he did not want me to feel that I was receiving favors.

My pride thus safeguarded, I eagerly accepted and had no reason to regret my decision.

The old man revealed himself to be a God-gifted teacher. He taught me not only the two languages I had wished to acquire; he taught me to think. Socrates must have used similar means in conversing with his disciples, prodding their wit with sharp questions and never allowing them to ask one that they could answer themselves.

Twice a week I wound my way to the narrow house. After a while I discovered that Eleazar shared it with two grown sons and a grandchild. I would encounter them on the stairs from time to time, but they never entered the library when I was there.

My diligence seemed to satisfy the old man. Maimonides

and *Avicenna yielded their secrets to me, but aside from those rewarding studies, I learned little* in praxi.

Of anatomical demonstrations, there were few. The procedure never varied: a barber-surgeon would open the corpse while, at a safe distance, the professor would read aloud the Galenic text, which more often than not had no bearing on what was being shown. Once, the barber held aloft a shinbone while the docens *was explaining the skull!*

As I learned nothing from those demonstrations, I worked for myself as best I could, dissecting dogs, cats, rats, and mice, observing how the same organ shows variations according to different species. Yet those were no more than clumsy attempts. I sensed that I had merely made a few chance discoveries but had not learned the foundations of the science.

Halevy sensed my impatience. One day he told me that from then on I was to be on my own in furthering my knowledge of philosophy and the ancient tongues. As for medicine, the University of Salamanca had nothing more to offer me.

"Go to Padua, my son," he told me, *"and study under Andreas Vesalius, in whose hands the sorely decayed art of healing is blooming anew."*

I agreed, and strove to be done with Salamanca as quickly as I could. I easily obtained a baccalaureate in medicine by parroting the egregious professors and participated in the graduation ceremonies, where the faculty, in full regalia, presides first of all over a bullfight. Then I took leave of my kind tutor, thanking him from the very bottom of my heart for all he had done for me.

"From the very bottom of his heart?" Vrone wondered.

"For a few Hebrew lessons? And he paid him, did he not? This sounds as if Eleazar had at least saved his life."

Miguel gave her a look.

"He did save his life, Veronica. My father had every reason to be thankful to the old bookworm. He does not mention the incident here, and small wonder."

"What happened?"

"Well, my father went to the churchyard one night to look for some bones . . ."

"*What?*" Her eyes widened.

"Certainly. What else could he do, with only three anatomy demonstrations a year and the hangman forbidden to sell dissection material? The Inquisition may torture and burn us when we are alive, but it worries a great deal about us once we are dead.

"So my father in the darkness was picking up a rib here, a pelvis there, when two soldiers of the Holy Office surprised him. There was a fight. He damaged them both rather severely and escaped, but with a gash from a halberd in his thigh — from the knee right up to the hipbone. Next day it was announced with drums to the townspeople to be on the lookout for a student with a limp who had, the night before, desecrated a grave and almost killed two faithful servants of the Inquisition's local chapter. My father, who had dressed his wound, forced himself to walk around straight; but in the evening, at Eleazar's house, he fainted. The cut had become infected. The old man put him to bed and for a fortnight took care of him. When he went out again, there was no outer visible trace of an injury. Had he been spotted, it would have meant the gallows."

"How lucky he was! Those two could have killed him in the churchyard!"

"Hardly." Miguel shook his head. "He was a consummate fencer. He learned the art from his father — the only useful thing, he often said, that he had ever learned from him. He passed it on to me."

"Are you good at it?"

"Tolerable." He laughed.

She had tried to make her question sound a little mocking, but could not help feeling a pleasurable shiver of admiration and fear running down her spine. It took her several moments to find the place on the sheet:

Then I left the banks of the Tormes, wondering how in the world I could persuade my father to send me to Padua.

It proved to be an easier task than I had feared. Again, Chacón was consulted. He supported my design. A few weeks later I was on my way to Italy.

I took the land route through France, for the sea between Barcelona and Genoa was, as it is now, alive with Moorish pirates, and my father knew that he could never afford the ransom were I taken prisoner by them. So it was many weeks before I rode into the bustling town.

What a difference from Salamanca! True, its center was the university, here as well as there, but while in the Spanish town foreign students were as rare as white crows, Padua's seat of learning attracted them in droves. A Babylonian confusion reigned, but no one felt a stranger, since Latin was understood by all, no matter how grossly it was sometimes pronounced.

Vrone laughed. "I expect that they all learned Italian rather quickly," she said.

"Oh yes, after a few weeks even the Muscovites are chatting away. Yet my father probably needed some time to get used to the Paduan way. The town is so unlike the ones in our homeland."

"How?"

"You see, a Spanish city is, on the whole, rather unwelcoming. We live in the inner courtyard of the house, behind grilled windows. And our walls and battlements seem to challenge the whole world. In Padua, people of all ranks consider the town's streets, alleys, squares, and bridges their domain, their forum. There they laugh, curse, sing, work, beg, talk, brawl, and bargain . . ."

Miguel fell silent. He saw his father, young, hesitant, and none too affluent, amid this boisterous crowd. Life and study in Padua must have been considerably harder for Juan de Roxas than they were to be for his well-provided, superbly prepared son. Yet never had he complained of past hardship to Miguel, but had always considered his Paduan days a sun-filled time. How understandable! Miguel suddenly felt impatient to be off. It would be six months, he remembered quickly, before he would be able to cross the Alps. He would go by Zürich and Chiavenna, he reflected; better avoid Geneva . . .

Vrone, sensing that his thoughts were straying, chose not to prolong the silence. She read on:

As my great good fortune would have it, Andreas Vesalius was still teaching anatomy in Padua that year. His classes were so crowded that one had to get up at cock's crow to secure a place.

Nowadays a physician is supposed to be well versed in anatomy. Everybody has studied the Fabrica, *and quite a few — though by no means all — of the human body's secret workings have been revealed.*

When I began my studies, however, Galen was still the

anatomists' bible, and whenever the "Prince of Physicians" was shown to be wrong, they would simply say that the human race had changed since Galen's time, and not for the better.

It was Vesalius who taught us to rely on our senses instead of blindly trusting Galen's every word and who brought back the use of the hands, which physicians had spurned and abandoned to unskilled barber-surgeons.

I shall never forget the day when I first heard him lecture.

We had gathered in a kind of amphitheater with ascending wooden benches. In the center, on a table, a cadaver was ready.

A young man came in, dark-eyed, with brown, curly hair and beard. He made straight for the corpse. He was followed by a servant carrying a mounted skeleton, which he propped up in front of the table. While I looked at those preparations, wondering where the cathedra was, why there were no barber-surgeons, and when Professor Vesalius at last would make his entrance, the young man seized a scalpel, made a swift incision, and began to talk.

"Use your eyes," he would say again and again.

Whatever part of the body he was dissecting, he would at once make us locate on the skeleton the sites of the organs and muscles he was showing us.

That day, he demonstrated the forearm muscles and how, after a long course, they end in the hand and in the joints of the fingers; how the muscles, in double layers, are situated one over the other, always four over four; how the lower ones tend to the first joint, the upper ones to the second and third joints, and always pass through the first one.

Then he took out the intestines and showed us the

*workings of the kidneys. The stench was nauseating, but
who cared? I learned more in this first session than I had
during the two years at Salamanca.*

Having finished the sheet, Vrone took the next one from
the stack of proofs.

JUAN DE ROXAS, VITA, SHEET TWO

*I studied with fervor. Yet even the most diligent scholar
needs recreation. Mine was to go to Venice whenever I
could afford it, which was not too often.*

*Inland-born, I marveled at this town built in the water,
where churches and palaces were reflected in a trembling,
ever-changing mirror. No less did I admire the sagacity of
its rulers, merchants who traded with the baptized and
unbaptized world, giving Caesar his due and accumulating
riches.*

Miguel smiled. "My father was enthralled by Venice,"
he remembered. "He told me that he would save his allowance for weeks on end, just to be able to hire a gondola
and to glide by those palaces with their marble fretwork,
sometimes at night by the light of a single torch . . ."

He stopped, wondering whether his father had discovered, as he had, that the black-veiled Venetian girls were
less inaccessible than their costume suggested. He was
unsure whether to smile at the thought or to be shocked by
its irreverence.

"A gondola" — Vrone interrupted his musing — "I
should like to ride in one, just once."

"It would please you. It is wonderfully soothing. It rocks
you softly, and the water blurs all lines."

"It must make you feel slightly drunk, does it not?"

"Yes, it does. But do you know? It does that only to
foreigners. They have the leisure to let their fancies roam.

The Venetians themselves never dream. They are merchants, men skilled at counting and weighing with precision, at gauging the true value of things beneath their surface. They have to keep their head in this realm of shifting shapes. No wonder Venice never had a poet."

Vrone smiled. "I don't think Toni would like that."

Miguel felt an inexplicable pinprick of jealousy. "Who is Toni?" he asked in a tone that he hoped was casual.

"Antonio Giunta. He is visiting printers here, hoping to pick up a few tricks of the trade." She rose and fetched a little book from one of the shelves. "Here."

It was the Giunta edition, exquisitely printed and bound, of Bernardo Tasso's *Amadis de Gaula*.

Antonio Giunta hopes that the Lyre of the Venetian Apollo will sound sweet to the ears of Basel's Minerva, the dedication read.

Miguel made a face. "Did you read the book?" he asked.

"No."

"Then how can you say that this Tasso is a poet?"

"I said nothing of the kind. I said, 'Toni won't like that.'"

His irritation mounted. "Why didn't you read the book?" he asked her.

"Because the first page bored me stiff," she replied.

He was impatient with the relief he felt. "Go on, Veronica," he said abruptly.

The studies are flowering, the spirits are stirring, off with you, O Barbarity, into exile!

A German colleague once read us those lines. We found them much to our liking. Had not the Emperor graciously accepted the dedication of the Fabrica, *the work of a man who indeed had used his eyes? Maybe mankind's childhood of superstition was about to end.*

Alas, though we had come to know more about the human body than anyone before us, we still had much to learn about human nature.

In 1544 I obtained my diploma and went back to Saragossa. My father received me cheerfully, which puzzled me, as I was bringing home a mere sheepskin and no prospects. Soon, however, I was enlightened as to the cause of his good mood: Daza Chacón had written to him that he had recommended me for employment on the Emperor's medical staff — albeit at a low rank — on completion of my studies. I was to depart for Brussels as soon as I came home. A hundred ducats, to defray the travel costs, were enclosed in the letter.

Apparently the doctor felt that he owed my father a good turn after having so recklessly encouraged me to follow the medical calling.

As my luck would have it, the Bishop of Monzón was about to go to Flanders. He gave me a place in his coach on the understanding that I would take care of him during his gout attacks. (Later I was to acknowledge the experience as a priceless apprenticeship in treating this affliction.)

I took leave of my parents. Fortified by their blessing and a little spending money I was on my way to the Emperor's court.

The poplar trees bordering the roads of France were already turning red and gold as we traveled northward, and one windy October day we rolled into Brussels. The next day I went to the castle to call on Master Chacón, who was summoned to see the Emperor after Mass. He took me with him.

Charles V at the time was forty-four years old, but I would easily have given fifteen more to the black-clad man sitting in an armchair, his gouty leg supported by a stool. He had just rung for a servant to push him nearer the window, for the morning mists had lifted and a pale blue sky was filling the arch. The ruler on whose kingdom the sun never set longed for the warmth of an autumn day's wan noon rays.

His face, lined and careworn, was not handsome, due to the strutting jaw only partly concealed by the beard, but his eyes, at once alive and sorrowful, made one forget such a small imperfection.

He beckoned us nearer. I was presented, and as Chacón was checking his pulse, the Emperor involved me in a light conversation while at the same time he satisfied himself as to my family and medical background. Then he dismissed us both, saying that he felt well and that he was confident of the skill of his physicians to drive away whatever sickness might befall him.

Out in the hall we encountered Vesalius, who, to my delighted surprise, remembered me from Padua. He welcomed me to the Imperial medical staff, but with a wry smile. I was to find out its meaning before too long: the Emperor turned out to be a trying patient.

He was frail of body and had been suffering from gout for many years. His stomach also gave him trouble. Yet although we could mitigate the gout attacks with warm baths and compresses, there was little to be done against his intestinal pains, for the Emperor, it must be said, was given to gluttony.

I often wondered about this curious weakness of an otherwise moderate and sober man, and concluded that the dinner table was the place he had chosen to give rein to his whims, for in his politics, more often than not, he had to bow to necessity.

He knew of this, his frailty, and would sincerely repent whenever he was tortured by stomach cramps after a breakfast of twenty oysters washed down with ice-cold beer, but would never change his ways, despite the entreaties of his physicians.

As the youngest member of his medical staff I could not advise a stricter surveillance of his eating habits, but one day I asserted myself against him while treating a different complaint.

A flea had bitten him on his left wrist. To relieve the itch, he had been scratching the spot until his hand and, indeed, his whole arm, were swollen to nearly twice their size.

He asked me whether I presumed to cure him of this torment.

"Indeed, I do," I replied, "if Your Majesty will promise me to follow my prescription to the letter."

This he did.

I now bandaged his right hand and fastened his right arm to his body. Then I put some clay paste on the sore and began my vigil, talking and reading to the patient, renewing the compresses, and refusing to remove the bandage from his arm to let him scratch. After two days the swelling subsided, and the Emperor showed himself delighted with my "Aragonese stubbornness," as he called it, which had withheld from him a momentary but harmful relief.

This little act of intransigence gained me his trust and favor, but vexed the Netherlanders at court, who were quick to fear a change in the precarious equilibrium between the Emperor's Flemish and Spanish retinue every time a Spaniard was added to the Imperial household.

They ought not have worried about my joining one of the numerous factions around the throne. Whenever my service did not keep me at the side of the Emperor, I was busy taking in the sights, sounds, and smells of Flanders, so different from those of my homeland.

In those days a Spaniard could still walk the streets of Brussels without fearing that a dagger might be planted between his shoulder blades at any moment.

I would stroll through the town, admiring churches and palaces, and even more the sumptuous houses of the burghers and the shops filled with merchandise from all four corners of the world. A finely dressed, well-fed crowd was bargaining and buying.

There were bolts of silk and linen, rolls of lace, furs, leather boots, gloves, plumed hats, weapons; there was Delft crockery, barrels of herrings, eels, and clams, wheels of cheese, garlands of sausages, basketfuls of red and yellow apples; there was a little shop where they sold eyeglasses, the rage of the day. The flower market was a sea of red, white, and yellow asters. There, in small burlap bags, you could buy tulip bulbs. (As it was the end of October, I had to wait until the following spring to see them bloom for the first time in my life.) Never had I seen such abundance, not even at the Merceria in Venice.

No wonder the Emperor set such store by this Land of Cockaigne. He would keep it within his kingdom, I knew, as long as he lived, for those debonair yet tough merchants were devoted to him. He spoke their language. Charles,

Fleming as much as Spaniard, had the right way with those two nations as disparate as water and fire. He knew their quirks; he catered to Spanish pride, yet respected Flemish privilege.

This delicate balance, however, was bound to the Emperor's person. I wondered what would happen after Charles's death. The Flemings would never tolerate a Spanish king, of this I was certain. Still, we would need them, I had to admit. It made me feel humiliated and ashamed.

Why, in the Devil's name, were we so poor? I asked myself. Why was the Emperor — our King — always in debt, in spite of the gold-laden caravels that kept coming from the New World?

Charles enjoyed close relations with Flemish bankers, who would sometimes lend him money at outrageous interest and, more often, give him good advice. Among them was Pieter Steen of Ghent, whose counsel and opinion the Emperor valued particularly.

"The Spaniards, Your Majesty," the old man said once, "are good only at grabbing. All their riches are loot. They do not understand how to work, how to make their money work."

Charles had stopped at Steen's town house, as he often did when in Ghent. He was now sitting by the fire in the latter's parlor, where everything, from the wall hangings to the exquisitely blown little cordial glasses, spoke of wealth. The Emperor had me in attendance because he was suffering again from gout.

"They never have learned how to wait. Look at them in the New World. They have worked the Indians to

*death in the silver mines. It escapes them that a slave has
to be fed and well treated to yield some return. They grab
and lose. Too bad, for they are courageous and hardy folk.
And far more charitable than our people." He chuckled.
"We do not like beggars. We tell them to go and earn their
keep. But the Spaniards are used to poverty, I fancy. That's
why they get so beside themselves at the sight of a mere
guilder."*

*I felt vexed. Old Steen had pointedly ignored my pres-
ence.*

*The Emperor, however, turned to me. Smiling sadly, he
said, "Would you care to answer this, Roxas?"*

*"As best I can, Your Majesty," I replied, pulling my
thoughts together. I spoke carefully. "Mynheer Steen says
that we Spaniards do not understand the laws of money
and trade. Maybe we were too busy to learn them, fighting
the Moors for seven hundred years."*

Steen agreed.

*"Also," I went on, "it was not our business. The Jews
and Moors took care of trade and finances until the Catholic Kings drove them out."*

"More's the pity," said Steen.

*"We are not half-wits," I said, somewhat heatedly. "We
can learn."*

*"Better hurry," Steen answered. "This is the reason, Your
Majesty," he went on, ignoring me again, "that it would
not be advisable to entrust the Duke of Alba with the
civilian government here. He is a great soldier, but I doubt
whether he is privy to the workings of our trade. He might
bend some delicate screws there and stop the wheels altogether."*

Miguel laughed. "Grandfather Steen never said such a thing. This is the expurgated version."

"*Grandfather* Steen?"

He nodded. "My father later on married Steen's granddaughter."

"Your great-grandfather, then."

"Yes, but that's too long to say each time."

"So — what *did* he say?"

"I think he said: 'Majesty, your Alba is a fool. Do not ever let him loose on Flanders. He would be bound to kill the goose that lays the golden eggs.' He's doing his best right now."

Vrone sighed. Basel was full of refugees from the Netherlands. Then she went on:

After the Emperor's death, this is precisely what happened. As I am writing this, we are losing our richest provinces and, what may be even worse, our counterpart, our alter ego. We and the Flemings — have we come to hate each other? It seems so, but I believe that we are rather mutually attracted, as opposites — and opponents — often are. We admire their stubborn toil, which has wrenched their fertile land from the sea — and they are amazed at our passion to fight lost battles. They want to see how long Spanish pride will hold out against Flemish obstinacy, for they know that they will win in the end. Yes, we will lose the provinces, but their memory will linger in the Spanish heart. Even our melancholy King, whenever he wants to look at strange things, chooses a Flemish madness: they say he likes the work of that crazed soul Hieronymus Bosch.

"Who is he?" Vrone asked.

"A painter. I've never seen any of his pictures, though. God knows what they look like."

Vrone let her eyes run down the sheet. A lot about the Emperor, she thought. I cannot wait until he comes to his marriage. How did this Pieter Steen ever consent to give his granddaughter to a penniless Spaniard? For penniless the young doctor must have appeared to the banker, salary or no.

She read:

At the time I came to Flanders, Charles was beset by many troubles. He was continually on the move, trying to deal with them. There was France, the Crescent; there were the German princes; there was, above all, the New Doctrine.

It was at Regensburg, where the Emperor had called the Diet in the hope of coming to terms with the Protestants, that I took a first look at Luther and his followers.

As a boy in Spain, I had heard of him as the embodied Antichrist. His books were burned, often enough along with those who had read them. Later, when I studied at Padua, my colleagues and I were more concerned with God's handiwork than with His word.

In Regensburg I read Luther's treatise on the Unfree Will — De servo arbitrio — which troubled me. I found it dangerous for the minds of the common folk, since it declared that man could not bring about his salvation by his own deeds and earnest striving. Good works were also declared useless. Indeed, there were then in Germany quite a few people busily doing nothing, waiting for Divine Grace to descend upon their empty heads.

Those of the German princes who were sworn to the New Doctrine had not come to Regensburg. A few weeks later, they attacked.

War, strange to say, had a curative effect on Charles. His fits of gout subsided whenever we were under fire. Save for longer sojourns at Brussels, where I lived at the castle, my sleeping quarters during the next ten years showed great variety: there were four-posters, camp beds, even berths aboard ships. When we fled from Innsbruck, Duke Maurice of Saxony at our heels, the sick Emperor carried in a litter, I slept for many a night on damp straw, and during the siege of Metz, that ill-fated and fruitless undertaking, my bed was the frozen ground.

Innsbruck and Metz! It looked as if Fortune was avenging herself on the man who had subdued her at Mühlberg when he beat the Protestant princes. Yet it was not an angry goddess's wrath that had brought distress upon the Emperor. It was his own doing. In war and politics, some blunders are fatal.

Puzzled, Vrone looked up. "What blunder, Miguel?"

"The bid for the succession. Charles wanted to secure the Imperial crown for his son, our present King. This infuriated everybody — the Flemings, the Germans, the Austrian cousins. They all hated Philip. His manner was cold and stiff. Father told me that the Emperor tried his damnedest to make his son unbend; even had him take drinking lessons! It did no good; Charles was looking for five feet in a cat, as we say at home . . . Within a few years, the princes rallied. They overran the Imperials, and Charles had to flee from Innsbruck."

"In a litter? Over the mountain? And no one going after

him on horseback?" Vrone shook her head at such ineffi-
ciency on the part of Duke Maurice. Then she read on:

*Vesalius and I took care of the Emperor in all those cam-
paigns. Ever the scientist, my illustrious colleague and former teacher would pursue his anatomical studies, unruffled
by the changing fortunes of war.*

*I remember him during our escape from Innsbruck.
Whenever our party reached a village, and a bed had been
found for the Emperor, together with some scrawny
chicken for a meal, Vesalius would head straight for the
churchyard to dig up skulls and examine them, for often
they differed greatly from those we had seen and studied
in Padua; and no wonder: strange kinds of men and women
lived in those mountains, misshapen both in mind and body,
with protruding eyes, slavering mouths, and goiters as big
as cabbages. Vesalius speculated that something in their diet
reduced them to such a state. He became so fired by the
question that he once offered a peasant two florins if the
latter would lend him, for a day or two, a certain Tobias
who lived in a dog hut by the farmhouse. He would treat
him well, Vesalius promised; just feed him certain victuals
to see whether the goiter would shrink.*

*The man refused, saying that the creature was worth its
weight in gold, since it watched the farmhouse better than
any dog and did heavy work without ever asking for wages,
and that he could not spare Tobias even for a single day,
and anyway, why did the gentlemen want to hex away
Tobias' goiter? This would not do at all, for then Tobias
would look like anybody else and maybe refuse to live in
a dog's hut and do dogs' work. Better to leave Tobias alone.
He knew what he knew, the peasant added: last night,*

walking by the churchyard, he had spied one of the gentle-men scratching for skulls.

The village priest, our interpreter, gave us a strange look, and we beat a hasty retreat. A few hours later our party pushed on to Villach.

Again, Vrone vented her indignation. "Vesalius must have been out of his mind! Why, they could have burned him to a crisp! And all for some stupid skulls and goiters! He probably was so busy using his brain that he forgot to use his head! What next?"

She took off her spectacles again, cleaned them fiercely, clamped them back on her nose, which was too delicate for the heavy steel frames, and continued:

JUAN DE ROXAS, VITA, SHEET THREE

The Emperor, having succeeded, God knew how, in pacifying Maurice, went back to Innsbruck and from there to Augsburg. At Augsburg he decided to recapture Metz, the town some German princes had bargained away to the French King.

As far as I knew, wars were always waged in the summer, since then the inclemencies of the enemy were not aggravated by those of the weather. To begin a siege in the middle of November seemed to me a rather reckless move, but the Emperor, advised by his generals, went ahead.

Winter had set in early that year. We arrived before Metz with sixty thousand men. The snow was two feet deep. The soldiers had to shovel it aside before they could dig holes in the frozen ground. There they would crouch, protected only by some straw against the bitter cold. Many of them were in tatters, their toes showing through the holes of their boots. They looked almost barefoot — no wonder the French came to call them "the Emperor's Apostles."

I shall not attempt to describe this futile and foolish siege — even after thirty years my blood boils whenever I think of it — but shall confine myself to telling of my task there, that of tending the wounded.

We had our hands full, I, Chacón, and a few others from the Emperor's medical staff. We all had become military surgeons, even I, who had but limited experience with gunshot wounds.

It was a common belief that injuries caused by bullets were poisoned, since lead was considered a toxic metal. Thus, every gunshot wound was either cauterized or drenched in boiling oil.

I am ashamed to say that we could have spared the poor soldiers this stupid torture had we but read the pamphlet the French King's surgeon had written on such injuries. He stated therein that there was no poison whatever in bullet wounds. Therefore, they could and should be treated with egg yolk or some other soothing matter. He had learned this, he noted, from experience, having run short of oil in one of his King's previous campaigns. He then saw that those he treated with egg yolk recovered, while those who had suffered the cauterizing iron were in a pitiful state indeed.

The Emperor, seeing his soldiers dying at the rate of three hundred a day, also learned that M. de Guise, the French commander-in-chief, had decided to blow up the town rather than allow the Imperials to enter it.

The siege was lifted and the Emperor returned to Brussels. He was broken and exhausted.

I attended him during the spring and summer of 1553.
Around that time he began to think of abdication, but not
before he had betrothed his son, our present King, to the
Queen of England, because he was enticed by the dream
of adding the British Isles to the Empire.

"The English Queen, Miguel?" Vrone interrupted herself. "I thought she was a virgin."

"Not the ruling one, Veronica, but Mary, the one before her. My father used to say that he was glad indeed that those two — Philip and Mary — had no children. Mary was the King's aunt, twelve years older than he and a dried-up prune."

Vrone laughed. "What became of her?"

"Not much. Philip left her after a year of marriage, I think. She lingered for another four, consoling herself by killing Protestants by the hundreds. Bloody Mary, they called her. Now it's Elizabeth's turn. She kills Catholics."

"Bloody Bess," said Vrone and read on:

Nothing was to come of it — the couple had no children.
During the summer there were negotiations with the
English ambassador as well as conferences with our repre-
sentatives in London. The Emperor was often feverish and
impatient, like one who fears that his time may be running
short.

On September the eleventh — I shall remember this date
as long as I live — Vesalius called me to his quarters and
told me that my countryman Miguel Servetus had been
arrested in Geneva. My heart sickened at the thought of
the unfortunate one, twice excommunicated and abandoned
by God and man in a foreign land. Vesalius remarked that
he had never understood why Servetus, a physician, had

*dabbled in theology and had insisted on discussing his
unprovable speculations with Calvin of all men! Neither of
us could comprehend Servetus' utter foolishness in having
gone to Geneva.*

*The next day I asked the Emperor for a leave of absence,
which he granted without questioning me as to my journey's destination. He may have guessed it.*

*Vesalius added generously to my travel purse and gave
me letters of recommendation to present to his friends in
Basel, among them Bartholomaeus Faber, the renowned
printer, who was to show himself an honorable man and
true friend in times of sorrow.*

Vrone looked up from her sheet, a bitter smile on her
lips. It made her seem suddenly older.

"Father still talks about Servetus," she said; "he still has
nightmares whenever he thinks of him. It happened before
I was born. Father was the only one to speak out for him
at the time. What a bunch of cowards the rest were . . .
Well, let's get it over with." She read fast, in a level voice:

*I knew that I would be unable to change the fate of the
hapless man. I merely hoped that I could bring him the
consolation — however small — of a fellow countryman's
visit.*

I arrived at Geneva on October 12.

*At the hostelry I had to give my name and surrender my
sword and dagger. At seven o'clock at night the town was
as quiet as a churchyard, since a curfew had been ordered.
It was forbidden to sing, to dance, to go out to dinner, even
to take a walk, but as I was in no mood for a stroll, I went
to bed and prepared myself for my audience with Calvin.*

*The following morning he received me in his house,
which seemed to me a trifle comfortable for such an austere*

131

man. He showed me the civility due to a properly accredited visitor.

All in his countenance was narrow: the thin, hooked nose, the pinched mouth, the hollow cheeks. His eyes burned like those of the damned.

Certainly I would be allowed to see Servetus, he said, but not alone. It so happened, he added, that he himself was going to the prisoner the next day; I would be welcome to accompany him there.

I went back to my hostelry. The innkeeper told me that Servetus had come by Geneva on his way to Zürich, whence he had intended to go to Italy — to Naples, to be exact — where he wanted to practice medicine among the Aragonese at court. He was unable to find a boat to get him across the lake the same day. As it was a Sunday — no wonder he could not find a passage then — he had the insane thought of going to church to hear Calvin preach. There he was recognized and arrested. When God wants to destroy a man, He robs him of his reason.

To this day I shiver when I think of the dungeon where they held him. They had even walled up the windows to keep him from talking to anyone. He was rotting away in this humid hole, sick, dirty, his eyes inflamed, his fine face deeply lined, his hair all white, and he was only a little over forty years old.

Calvin immediately engaged him in a lengthy discussion that I did not follow, horrified as I was at the state of the prisoner. Finally he assured Servetus that he did not harbor any grudge against him; that he forgave him willingly.

"Forgave him for what?" Vrone asked.

"For some complicated error. I believe it had to do with the Trinity. As if it mattered . . ."

Such meekness, I knew, was an ill omen.

I came forward and embraced Servetus while Calvin watched us closely. We talked in Aragonese, which soothed the unfortunate man; he had not used his mother tongue for so long. He spoke for a while, mostly about his friends, and was touched by Vesalius' solicitude. His lot was cast, he knew, so he thanked me for my visit and asked only that I be present when they led him to the scaffold. The poor man was still hoping for beheading.

A few days later, the verdict was pronounced: the fire.

On the morning of October 27 they brought him out to the stake at Champel and bound him to an iron rod, his books heaped around him. He had been condemned to die by slow fire, but the crowd, indignant at this added torture, threw heavy logs into the flames. Thank God the smoke suffocated him within a short time.

Back in Brussels I went at once to see Vesalius. He merely nodded as I told him my dreadful tale.

"You can move a tiger to pity," he said, "even a king or a tyrant — but never a schoolmaster bent on defending his twaddle."

The next year the Emperor went to war for the last time against France. He had become so thin and wan that his armor rattled on him, although he was wearing a quilted jacket underneath it.

I shall not repeat my tales of gunshot wounds and other miseries; at least there were no chilblains, because the campaign took place in June. It was not successful. Charles soon returned to Brussels, where he intended to spend the fall and winter.

In July 1554 I married Marguerite Steen, Pieter Steen's

133

granddaughter. The Emperor was very pleased. Our wedding seemed to him a portent of hope for a future where Flemings and Spaniards would live in peace. He added a thousand escudos to my wife's dowry and told us that, as a townsman of the bride, he insisted on being godfather to our first child.

"That's all?" Vrone sounded disappointed.

"Well, not exactly. But, you see, my father was a rather private man. Besides, he never talked much about my mother. She died young."

"When?"

"Twelve years ago."

"Your father did not remarry?"

"No."

Vrone leafed through the remaining sheets and nodded. "I thought so," she said.

"Thought what?"

"This Vita has no entries after the year '68."

"Are you sure? Are there no pages missing?"

"No. Why should there be?"

"Why, my father lived for twelve more years!"

"But don't you see?" His incomprehension distressed her. "His life ended the day your mother died. From then on, he didn't care so much about what was happening in the world."

"Oh, yes, he did," Miguel protested. "He would talk to me for hours about the troubles in France, in Spain . . ."

"He would talk to *you*," she pointed out patiently; "he lived through you, for you. Had he been alone, he would not have given a straw about anything."

Miguel frowned.

He lived through you, for you. He thought of his father's

fervent, unrelenting attention, which, at times, had felt like a burden on his young shoulders. He was ashamed at the thought and angry at Vrone's guess.

"How do you know?" he asked her curtly.

"Because with *my* father, just the opposite happened. *He* came back to life as soon as my stepmother had made her exit."

"Made her . . . ?"

"Exit," Vrone repeated, unruffled. "You see, my own mother was a little older than my father. I was only ten years old when she died. He thought he needed a wife again and a mother for his child . . ." She shook her head. "But there was nothing but screams and broken pots in this house from the day she arrived. The whole town laughed at it. There even was a song going round:

> When I brought home my fresh young wife
> She beat me black and blue;
> O pray, dear Death of Basel,
> Give me back my old shrew!

"The press went downhill; my father was wretched. He would look at me sometimes as if he wanted to ask my forgiveness. I stayed in the shop more than in the house. She didn't mind; she cared no more about me than she cared about the work. She called it 'that dirty business,' but I liked it. I looked around and learned. She was just glad that I wasn't underfoot. That was when my father began to teach me Latin and Greek. She died in '74, when we had the plague here. From then on, my father came alive again. I guess a man's life changes one way or another when he loses his wife — depending on what she meant to him."

While Vrone spoke, Miguel turned the manuscript's pages one by one. The pagination was correct. Juan de Roxas had not bothered to describe the last twelve years of his life. Miguel asked himself how he had never seen the world-weariness in the older man's eyes. His conscience corrected him immediately. He had seen it, again and again, but, basking in his father's deep attention, or even petulant from time to time at too much solicitude, he had chosen to ignore it.

Vrone, sensing his mood, hastened to dispel it. "Tell me, how did he meet your mother?"

He brightened a little. "One day Pieter Steen suffered a stroke. On hearing of it, the Emperor sent my father to look after him. My mother, eighteen at the time, was taking care of the old man. She and the doctor must have held a conference in the sickroom . . ."

Vrone laughed.

"Pieter Steen was to say later that this free treatment had cost him dearly, since the physician walked away with his granddaughter. But he came to like my father. He also appreciated the Imperial favor and predicted that Marguerite's children would be governors and generals."

Vrone winked at Miguel and read on:

JUAN DE ROXAS, VITA, SHEET FOUR

After the wedding I again assumed my duties at court. My wife joined me there, which pleased the medical staff, since our often intractable patient would take his pills and drafts quite meekly from her. In time a son was born to us.

"So you have a brother!" Vrone exclaimed.

"No. I *had* a brother. He died before I was born."

There was a slight pause. Vrone would have liked to ask

what had caused the boy's death, but Miguel did nothing to encourage her. Farther on, the manuscript might mention it, she thought, and continued:

The Emperor, true to his word, held the squalling child over the baptismal font in Brussels' Castel Chapel while we watched with bated breath lest he drop it from his gout-stiffened hands.

Indeed, his health was declining, but it was more a sickness of the soul than of the body, for he saw that the travails of his lifetime had come to naught: France was more powerful than ever, the Turks ruled over the Mediterranean and the peace he had wrenched from the Lutherans at Augsburg was no more than a precarious truce — no bulwark against the storms of the time.

I knew that he would abdicate the throne within a few months — he often talked to me about it — but I kept my counsel until his decision became official.

In the great hall of the castle, a solemn gathering was waiting. Governors, councillors, the Knights of the Golden Fleece, the representatives of the Flemish Estates, delegations of the towns of Flanders, the high and low clergy, the members of the Imperial household.

Prince Philip stood near the throne with the Duke of Alba.

The Emperor, dressed in mourning, appeared with halting steps, leaning on the arm of the Prince of Orange. He began to speak. After enumerating all his toils, travels, and campaigns, he declared that extreme fatigue forced him to surrender his lands unto his son Philip and to place the Empire into the hands of his brother Ferdinand.

"I have never," he concluded, "intentionally infringed

on the rights of anyone. If I have done so, I ask forgiveness."
At this, everybody wept.

*Prince Philip came forward. He apologized for being
unable to speak Flemish and said that the Bishop of Arras
would read a proclamation for him. This did not please the
audience. They dried their tears and listened in silence.*

*A few months later the Emperor retired to a Hierony-
mite monastery near Yuste in Estremadura. He had considerably reduced his household, but kept me as his personal physician. With my wife and little son I followed him
to Spain.*

We were to live in Yuste for two peaceful years.

*Charles had a little villa built for himself and his closest
retinue: his Gentleman of the Bedchamber, Don Luis
Quixada, the Sieur van Male, Dr. Mathys, and myself. My
wife and son lived in the village, for, strange to say, the
Emperor sometimes had fits of misogyny and would not
look at any woman, not even at the crone who came for the
laundry, though at other times he would invite Marguerite
to dinner, and their Flemish conversation would be cheerful
and lighthearted.*

*Living in monastic quiet, tending his flower beds, he
would nevertheless follow the events in the world. Messengers came and went, as well as visitors.*

*One day Don Luis brought an eleven-year-old boy to
see the Emperor — a handsome, bright, and cheerful lad.
He was the son of the beautiful Barbara Blomberg of Regensburg. She had been Charles's last love. In due time the
youngster would become Don Juan de Austria, Great
Admiral of the Fleet and victor at Lepanto.*

Don Carlos, the Crown Prince, also called on the Em-
peror. His visits, however, would leave Charles in such
gloom that it sometimes took days before he could find
pleasure again in his books and flowers.

Vrone lifted her eyes from the sheet. "It looks to me," she
said, "as if this Carlos was less handsome, bright, and cheerful, right?"

"Indeed. I once saw him ride into Saragossa at an opening
of the Aragonese Crown Council; that is, he did not ride,
but was crouched on the horse, holding on for dear life
while a groom led the mount by the rein. He passed six
feet from our balcony, and I still remember how shocked
I was at his face. Everyone would have recognized him as
Charles's grandson, even I, who was no more than seven
years old and knew the Emperor only from the portrait
sketch we had at home. Yet it seemed that some devil had
amused himself by distorting Charles's features, making the
jutting jaw still longer, the lower lip yet thicker, the pallor,
chalky and the eyes (those of the Emperor, according to
my father, were blue and full of life), the eyes dull brown
and froglike. To boot, he was rickety, with one shoulder
higher than the other, and was said to be half-witted. My
mother wept as she watched the prince and his cortège go
by, and my father looked as if he, too, would have liked
to cry. There were rumors that Carlos' favorite pastime
was to roast squirrels and rabbits alive. I daresay the Emperor must have been disturbed whenever he saw him."

"Well, he made his own bed," Vrone declared, unmoved.
"Why didn't he change his will in favor of this Juan?
That's what old Froben did. There was only one son, Jürg.
The girls had married away. Jürg drank like a fish. He

would have run the firm into the ground in no time. So, what do you know, out of the blue, old Froben brought forth a boy he had had some fifteen years before by a scullery girl. The lad had grown up in a monastery and was supposed to enter the Church. Froben put him into the workshop and legitimized him. The boy did well, and when his father died and they opened the will, they found that the business had been written over to Erasmus Froben. That's what the old man had named his son — Erasmus. After the Rotterdamer. *He* had been a love-child too."

Vrone giggled, and Miguel could not help laughing, too. "Erasmus married and had a clutch of children. He is still alive, high in his seventies. Two of his sons are running the press."

"Your competitors, then."

"Oh, no," Vrone conceded generously. "They are more in the scholarly field."

"Aren't you?"

"Yes, but only so far as the trade books pay for it. If I bring out, say, a volume of Lucretius, I must price it moderately so that poor students can afford it. My profit comes from cookbooks and calendars with silly pictures, things that everybody buys."

Miguel leaned back in his chair and laughed again. The folk in the printing business had to rise early indeed to get the better of Veronica Faber. How Pieter Steen would have liked this girl!

He almost forgot to turn his page as Vrone read on:

Everything comes to its end. One afternoon the Emperor, sitting on his balcony, was seized by a chill. He had a little fever and took to his bed. He saw Death coming. The Requiem was sung while Charles, holding a crucifix, re-

ceived the Last Rites. There was silence. Suddenly we heard the Emperor's voice, loud and clear: "Ay, Jesús!" He had passed away.

I was now appointed court physician to King Philip, according to the Emperor's expressed wish.

Madrid's "six months of winter and six months of Hell" proved fatal to our little Carlos. The following year he died of the croup. My wife's prostration and fragile health caused me to seek my release from royal service. At first, the King refused. But Vesalius, our friend and Marguerite's countryfellow, spoke for me and succeeded in making the King change his mind. We left court and capital for Saragossa, where we settled in the old town house, my parents having died in the meantime.

A year later, on Michaelmas Day, my wife was delivered of another son, who was baptized hastily by a mere midwife.

This one, thank God, passed unscathed through his childhood diseases and grew into young manhood. At this writing he is pursuing his medical studies at Padua.

In those years I divided my time between my practice and my studies. The question of the exchange between arterial and venous blood intrigued me, and I wanted to take up where Servetus had left off. I also wanted to learn more about muscle reflexes under metallic influence in dead bodies, for I thought that such knowledge could be used in the treatment of epileptics; but this was impossible, dissection having been recently forbidden by royal decree.

Off with you, O Barbarity, into exile . . .

It had returned with a vengeance. I often talked about

this with Vesalius, who would call on us whenever the court sojourned in Aragón. At the time, he was preparing to seek his freedom, for he had learned that at Padua the chair of anatomy had become vacant by the death of Fallopius. In 1564 he stopped at our house on his way to the Holy Land, where he was going, he said, to atone for some unspecified sin.

JUAN DE ROXAS, VITA, SHEET FIVE

The pious King had given him permission to leave Spain for this pilgrimage. We smiled, knowing that his thoughts were on quite another Jerusalem. He was never to reach it: a few months later he was shipwrecked in the Mediterranean. We had seen him for the last time.

Later, rumor had it that by mistake he had cut open a still-living person and that this was the crime he sought to expiate by his voyage to Palestine. This is nonsense. His skill would have precluded such a blunder. However, there may be an explanation for this foolish story: a few muscles may have twitched at the approach of the knife, as sometimes happens in fresh cadavers, enough to send some ignorant bystander racing off with a tale of horror.

In 1565 my old mentor, Eleazar Halevy, moved to Saragossa with his family. Aragonian privileges seemed to warrant a safer abode here than in the old university town, where Jews, Moors, and Marranos were more closely watched. He came to see me two times, bringing an orphaned little girl with him. While I was visiting with the old man, who had become frail indeed, Marguerite befriended the motherless child. He died shortly afterward. I never saw any of his sons again. They must have left the kingdom.

The manuscript slid from Miguel's hands.

Vrone stopped.

Unseeing, his lips pale, he was staring past her.

"Miguel, Miguel, what is it?"

"They did not leave the kingdom." His voice was tone-less. "They stayed, the fools. It will blow over . . . Nothing is eaten as hot as it is cooked . . ."

She had the wit to refrain from questions.

"It tallies, Veronica. Two old men and a grown woman with a child. God knows who had sired the brat," he added with sudden savagery. He could not bring himself to pity the victims — not at that moment. Their self-deceiving inertia had brought about their destruction and they had dragged his father down with them. "Two old men . . ." he repeated. "No wonder Paca knew them." He fell silent again, seeing it all.

For years those Jews had been living in Saragossa, sub-dued, nearly invisible, in the absurd hope that they could wait out the storm. But then, one day, Padre Domingo had arrived in town and had vowed to smoke out Jews, Moors, and Conversos alike. The wall gates were probably watched while he staged his mock trial. The Halevys must have come to Juan de Roxas for protection. "In the dead of the night," Paca had said. His father had paid a debt of gratitude. At the same time, Vega, eyeing the house, had seized the opportunity to involve the doctor in the proce-dure, to bring the recluse to the attention of the Holy Office.

But who had denounced him? Who knew that Juan de Roxas was concealing those wretches in his wine cellar? Not Vega. He would have had him arrested, forgoing the comedy of calling him as a witness for the Crown. Camacho? Unlikely. He stood to gain from silence, since he could count on ransoming the fugitives a few days later, when vigilance at the gates had slackened and they might try to reach the mountains. Paca? Never. Though she had disapproved of hiding the Jews, she would have died on the rack rather than betray the doctor. Who, then?

Miguel pressed his palms against his throbbing temples. Worried, Vrone looked at him and gathered her sheets together. "Miguel," she said, "this should do for today."

He started. "No." He spoke harshly. "Let's finish. It is only half a page."

"Whatever you want."

In 1567 we traveled to Ghent with our young son for a visit with Pieter Steen. It was to be the old man's last joy. He died at Christmas of that year and thus was spared the sorrow of seeing his old misgivings justified: In May 1568 the King sent an army into the Netherlands. Its commander was the Duke of Alba.

In September of the same year my wife died of a colic fever.

I have come to the end of my tale. Looking back on my life, I see, astonished, that this raging century has allowed me to partake of its glories, yet has shielded me from its furors. My sorrows — the death of my wife and of my first-born son — were at least God-ordained, not decreed by tribunals of blood and fire.

Shall I be spared to the end? Or shall I be called to bear witness to my truth, as were the many whose shadows rise before me? If this should come to pass, I shall act what-

ever way I can. God help me, then, that I not be found wanting.

> Juan de Roxas
>
> *At Saragossa, June the twentieth,* A.D. *1580*

In the fading light of the late winter day they had to strain their eyes over those last lines.

For a long while neither of them spoke. Dusk had yielded to darkness. Vrone sensed that Miguel was shivering, yet he did not stir. He needed comfort, she knew, but her solicitude would only have exasperated him. So she rose and took a pile of manuscripts from the far end of the table.

"I need to work on these tonight," she said; "they are too heavy for me to carry."

She walked to the door, opened it, and stepped out of the shop. His arms full of paper, he followed her.

The night was starless and stormy, but from across the alley a candle in Babeli's kitchen window shone like a small golden beacon over a sea of darkness.

ing, queen, nine and three . . ."

The candlelight flickered over the cards spread out on the kitchen table. With her gnarled, swollen finger the old woman poked king and queen in their flat, triangular faces.

"Look, Vroneli, it's coming out!"

"It's always coming out, Bab." Vrone sighed wearily. "Remember when old Brechbühler married? You had twins for him in the cards."

"How was I to know that he would break his neck before he could make them?" Babeli defended herself. "Besides, *she's* still alive, now, isn't she? You just wait."

"There's nothing to wait for, Bab," Vrone said, applying the advice to her own concern. "He doesn't care two pins for me. And even if he did, what could he do here? There are doctors enough in Basel as it is. He's going back to Padua."

"And a good thing it is," Babeli replied. "He's just a vagrant who thinks he's doing you a favor by taking your money!"

Vrone's eyes flashed.

"He's not taking any money. He's earning it — every bit! The way he works, he'd deserve twice as much as I'm paying him. And don't you ever call him a vagrant!"

Babeli remained unruffled.

"Why don't you pay him more, then?" she asked innocently.

Why indeed?

He was an asset to the firm. His Latin and Greek were flawless, his eye unerring. Vrone would not have begrudged a higher salary to a corrector of his caliber. Why, then, was she so glad that he contented himself with such paltry wages? Was it, perhaps, because it would take him longer to get his tuition together?

Involuntarily, she smiled. This was not lost on her old ally. "Vrone," Babeli asked, taking the dilemma by the horns, "have you truly hung your heart on him?"

Soberly, the girl nodded. "It looks like it."

"Too bad," Babeli remarked. "I would have liked to see you marry the Froben boy."

Vrone gave her a wry look. Babeli would marry her off to a different wealthy Basler every month, but those wishes would never come true. Vrone would rather run her printing press than a spinning wheel. For quite a while there had been no suitor asking Bartholomaeus Faber for the hand of his daughter.

"It won't be easy," Babeli reflected.

Vrone looked up sharply. Her own mind, bravely rational, had dismissed any chance of ever marrying Miguel. Now Babeli, who had a way of knowing things, seemed to tell her that the remote was not the impossible.

"There will be trouble . . ." Babeli spoke slowly, as if she were an oracle. "I saw it coming . . . such a good-looking one. His father came through here, years ago. That's why I felt I knew the young one . . . He's the spitting image . . . save for the eyes . . ."

"Tell me about his father, Bab."

"There's not much to tell — he was sick. All worked up over that miscreant down in Geneva. So was Master Barthel. To speak of him . . . he'll be the least of our worries . . ."

Vrone sat still, waiting for the verdict.

"You must be patient, Vroneli, and you mustn't, for anything, let him guess that you're eating your heart out. It would make him run to the far end of the world. And now let's have another look." She swept the cards together.

But Vrone put her delicate hand with the black-rimmed nails (all her scrubbing never could get out the printer's ink) on Babeli's and the pack of cards at once.

"No, Bab," she said. "I'd rather go to bed. I'll have to be up tomorrow at the crack of dawn."

"Why?"

"Driving to the paper mill. Good night."

"You'll take him along?"

"What if I do? He's never been in a sleigh, I'm sure. They have little snow in Spain."

"And showing yourself off with him, bells a-tinkling?"

"It's his horse."

"No, it isn't. Has he not made you a present of it?"

Vexed, Vrone opened the door, ready to slam it shut behind her, when Babeli spoke again. "You're no cook, Vrone Faber. A dough needs to rest."

The girl looked at the old woman who, smiling, put her finger over her lips. Then she left the kitchen, gently closing the door.

On Faber's night stand, next to a burning candle, sat an iron pot filled with steaming flour paste. With a spatula Miguel was busy spreading the mixture on a piece of linen. As soon as the rag was covered, he wrapped it around

Bartholomaeus' narrow chest, securing it with a second bandage. Then he cautiously lowered the patient onto his back and pulled the featherbed up to his chin.

The printer was suffering from the catarrh, which overcame him every winter. Vrone and Babeli had been with the sick man all day but had now gone to bed, leaving him, as the girl said, "in the expert care of his Paduan doctor."

"Too hot, Master Faber?"

"Just right. What clever hands you have, Miguel. Where did you learn to make such exemplary poultices?"

"At the *clinicum* in Venice, Master Faber. Acqua demands that one spend at least six months at the hospitals there to learn the craft, from splinting fractures to amputations . . . Why, he even has us pull teeth," Miguel added, with laughing indignation.

"I commend him. There should be a skilled Samaritan in every physician worth his salt, no matter how great a scholar he is."

"That's what Vesalius said."

"True, he said it. But with Andreas, thirst for knowledge came before the care of his ailing fellow man. He was an incomparable scientist, but he was not the healer your father was."

"Yet my father did not come to medicine because he wanted to help the sick, Master Faber. He came to it through a sense of wonder," Miguel observed. He stretched out his arm, on which the shirt sleeve was rolled back, bent it, and watched the play of his young muscles, trying to capture his father's awe at the sight of the cadaver's limb moving up.

"Granted," Faber replied, "but every bit of knowledge he gained he would use to get the better of pain and death.

149

He hated the suffering of the flesh." Though feeble and hoarse, Faber's voice conveyed fierce approval. "When he passed through here on his way back from Geneva, he was heartsick and spent. At the time, Agnes — my wife — was down with the murr. Dr. Veggli had given up on her. Your father insisted on taking over. There was no sleeping for him anyway, he said, what with the nightmare lying in wait for him whenever he closed his eyes. He pulled her through."

Faber stopped, a dry cough racking his chest and throat.

Miguel pulled back the coverlet and checked the bandage. Too tight, maybe? It would not do to compress the lungs, to impair respiration; Faber's breathing was already too shallow. He loosened the linen strips. A grateful look from the sick one moved him strangely. He had grown fond of this frail, gently clever man, and he hoped — for the first time with a touch of humility — that his skills would enable him to help his father's friend.

Faber, his cough subsided, resumed his recollections.

"One day the Reverend Wyss from Saint Catherine, on hearing of my wife's illness, came by and said that God educated us through suffering. Your father" — he chuckled — "your father told him that most people got more education than they would ever need, and showed him the door."

Miguel nodded. He could well see his father making short shrift of this officious man of God who was plaguing his patient. Under his hands Agnes Faber and many others had recovered from sickness, but he had been powerless to save his own wife.

To be sure, the murr, as Bartholomaeus called it, a lung congestion, could be cured with luck, but a colic fever

killed the patient within twenty-four hours. Juan de Roxas
seldom talked about Marguerite and would never mention
her fatal illness. It was Paca who had told Miguel about his
mother's last hours in pain and fever, how her lower body
had been so swollen and tender that she could not even
tolerate the weight of the blanket anymore, and how
Doctor Juan, to the faithful servant's indignation, had
refused to administer a cathartic, a needless torture he had
said. "Your mother died the same night. Who knows, perhaps a purge of honey might have helped her." Miguel had
shaken his head, convinced that his father had done the right
thing. But how could anybody be certain? It was out of
the question to dissect the body. Spiritual and secular
authorities in Spain looked askance at the practice, and
Paca, horrified, would not have kept silent.

The past year, however, he had observed similar symptoms — fever, pain, a swollen abdomen — when Monna
Bice, the laundress, sickened and died within a few hours.
Since she had been poor and no one had claimed the body,
she had ended up on the anatomy table. The autopsy
showed that a part of the intestine, the vermiform appen-
dix, had been inflamed and had ruptured, poisoning the
whole peritoneum with pus. At the time he had made a
mental note to mention those findings to his father at the
next vacation. Confirming the hopeless diagnosis Juan de
Roxas had made at the time might have taken away a last,
lingering, tormenting doubt, putting his father's mind at
rest.

But there were so many exciting things to relate, and
Juan de Roxas had been in such an unusually cheerful
mood, that Miguel was reluctant to see the all-too-familiar

frown of grief appear between his father's eyebrows and had postponed talking about the painful subject until the last day.

That evening a servant of the Montoyas had come with a note from Don Fernando, inviting father and son to a farewell dinner across the square. It was not a time to talk about Marguerite's sickness and death. And the next morning, his foot in the stirrup, Miguel had decided to leave the matter until the next vacation.

Regret too bitter for tears engulfed him, a sorrow altogether different from the distress he had felt during the last months.

Faber, puzzled by the silence, opened his eyes. They rested on the young man sitting motionless by the bed, staring into the candle flame.

March arrived and began melting the icicles hanging from the eaves above Miguel's garret window.

One night a loud, grinding noise woke him. He jumped up and opened the shutters. A balmy wind blew into his face. The noise had ceased. Leaning over the sill, Miguel looked at the congregation of gabled roofs, separated by the aisle of the ice-covered Rhine. In their midst the two prickly spires of the cathedral — not twins; rather an older and a younger brother — stood in the uncertain light of a waxing moon, every so often revealed, then hidden by fleeting clouds. The Good Town of Basel.

Within its walls, Juan de Roxas had found solace and friendship while on a heartbreaking errand. Years later it had given asylum to his son.

Yet gratitude alone, Miguel guessed, did not account for

his reluctance to leave this place. What had become of his studies? What business did he have lingering in this complacent, welcoming town, so comforting to the fugitive, with its sturdy, half-timbered houses warmed by round, green-glazed tile stoves, with its secluded squares, each with a fountain in the middle now releasing no more than a steady drop that hollowed out the ice mound beneath it?

When had he last attended an anatomy demonstration? Quick, which were the nerve pairs branching out from the cerebellum? It took him a while to name them.

It was high time for him to leave, before his heart grew any more of those tiniest roots which were beginning to cling to the town's very cobblestones.

He was now making five florins a week. At such a rate, he would soon have earned the sum necessary for his tuition. Come June, he would be gone, even if it meant the Bursa.

The wind had blown away a few heavy clouds. The crescent moon stood bright above the town.

In future years he would often come back and visit, Miguel thought. Old Faber then would be a little more frail, but still gentle and bright, and Veronica would be married. This latter notion, however, he found improbable on second thought. Veronica Faber, bespectacled, business-minded, and almost twenty, was headed for spinsterhood. The prognosis gave him an odd satisfaction.

Again the crunching noise broke the stillness. It seemed to come from the river. He strained his eyes: there were deep cracks in the dull mirror. He dressed, stole out of the house, and ran down to the steep bank.

A little later the night watchman, calling out the eleventh

hour, pointed to his head and shook it in disapproval as he saw a young man leaning over the parapet of the Rhine bridge, shouting encouragement to each ice floe breaking loose from the huge, frozen sheet, and applauding when it glided away on the black waters.

A blue spring sky filled the open window of the workroom. Stillness reigned: the press in the adjacent hall was at rest. Printers, composers, and apprentices, generously released by Mistress Faber in the early afternoon, had all gone to the yearly shooting match on the Rhine field.

Sitting at the table covered with galley proofs and woodcuts of plants, Miguel and Vrone, armed with scissors, red pencil, and glue, were busy at the layout for the new herbal the firm was bringing out, an abbreviated version of Leonhart Fuchs's detailed and cumbersome work *De Historia Stirpium*. Bartholomaeus had hired a professor from the university to write brief explanations of the pictures, but the man had been carried away by his own erudition. His comments were even more long-winded than the original. Miguel and Vrone, wielding their weapons with glee, clipped the prose and pondered the fate of every expendable subspecies.

"*Bellis perennis seu pratensis*," Vrone read.

"Away with it. We already have *margarita pratensis*. It's the same flower, only larger."

Miguel sent a sheet of paper sliding across the table, the proof of a woodcut. It showed a daisy in full bloom.

"*Margarita pratensis* . . . Marguerite. That was your mother's name, was it not?"

"Yes. Marguerite Ghislaine."

With her pencil Vrone retraced the delicate petals. "Tell me — what was she like?"

He leaned back and thought for a while. "She was a dancer," he finally said.

"A dancer? A merchant's daughter?"

"Forgive me, I meant to say that she was light on her feet. I was no more than seven years old when she died, but that is the way I remember her. You can recognize persons from afar, not by their face, but by their walk. My mother hardly touched the ground." He was silent for a moment. "We had an orchard near the Gallego. Once we drove out there for the *feria*, the fair of San Martin. My mother learned to dance the *jota* in no time."

"The *jota*?"

"Yes, the *jota Aragonesa*." He said it with sudden pride. "The villagers did not believe their eyes. The next morning they presented her with *alpargatas* — canvas slippers — made to measure from a left shoe of hers they had filched somehow. The cobbler had worked on them during the night. From then on, they said, she would never be without footwear, for whenever a pair was danced through, which would be soon, they hoped, a new one would be awaiting her. It never was to happen — she died a few months later. That first pair still hung on her bedroom wall, the rope soles barely used."

There was a pause.

Then Vrone spoke hesitantly. "The *jota* — is it difficult?"

"Very," he replied, smiling.

Her heart was pounding in her throat. "Show me."

"Show you the *jota*?"

"If you don't mind."

She bent her head. A sun ray made a little crown of her topknot.

"Without drums or fifes?"

"Can't we make our own music?"

Her eagerness amused him. "I guess we can," he replied. "First the drummer: *one*, two, three, *one*, two, three, *one*, two, three . . ."

He had seized a pair of scissors and was rhythmically beating their twin heads against the table top. "Your turn." He handed them to her.

One, two, three, *one*, two, three, *one*, two, three . . .

"Keep on. I'll clap a *jota*. Keep drumming."

One, two, three, *one*, two, three, *one*, two, three . . .

Clapping his hands against the scissors' steady beat, he played with it, teased it, giving way, then catching up with the unyielding pulse. Whenever the downbeat passed unacknowledged or the measure's weakest part was suddenly topped with an accent, their eyes met in joyful collusion.

One, two, three, *one*, two, three, *one*, two, three . . .

> "*Como quieres que te de*
> *Lo que no te puedo dar . . .*"

It flashed through her mind that she had never heard him speak, let alone sing, in his native tongue. Although subdued, his voice gloried in it.

> "*La cinta de mi sombrero*
> *Si no la puedo quitar . . .*"

She had put the scissors aside and was now clapping her hands, fingers against hollow palm, letting the willful *jota* weave in and out the pulse.

One, two, three, *one*, two, three, *one*, two, three . . .

> *"La cinta de mi sombrero*
> *Si no la puedo quitar . . ."*

Timidly, to his encouraging smile, she repeated the last two lines with him. Clapping, they sang the verse together:

> *"Como quieres que te de*
> *Lo que no te puedo dar*
> *La cinta de mi sombrero*
> *Si no la puedo quitar . . ."*

One, two, three, *one*, two, three, *one*, two, three . . .

> *"Sol y luna, luna y cielo*
> *Donde estuviste a noche*
> *Que mis ojos no te vieron . . ."*

Singing, he jumped up, kicked a few chairs out of the way, and before she knew it had turned the *jota* loose.

Spinning and leaping, his head thrown back, his fingers snapping in cadence, Miguel seemed for a moment to have forgotten his pupil, who involuntarily had straightened up as she watched him.

He stopped, not even catching his breath. "Ready, Veronica?"

She rose and stood facing him. "What do I do?"

"Just what I'm doing." He laughed. "The *jota* is a mirror dance! By the way, your skirt is too long."

She snatched the scissors from the table and cut off five inches from the hem.

"That's better," he approved. "Now take off your spectacles; otherwise, they'll fall off your nose. And get rid of your shoes."

She kicked off her clogs, then lifted her arms over her head as she had seen him do. "But I can't snap my fingers the way you do."

"You'll learn," he assured her.

Annoyed at finding herself blushing, she wondered whether he understood the implication of that last remark.

> "*Co-mo quie-res que te de
> Lo que no te pue-do dar*"

Slowly he taught her the steps. "Right — left — right — keep jumping. Land on both your feet!

> "*Como quieres que te de
> Lo que no te puedo dar
> La cinta de mi sombrero
> Si no la puedo quitar . . .*"

She moved with ease.
"Bravo! Here we go."

> "*Sol y luna, luna y cielo
> Donde estuviste a noche
> Que mis ojos no te vieron . . .*"

"Don't watch your feet, watch me!"

The command unsettled her. By keeping her eyes down, she had hoped to check the confusing, frightening, delightful feeling in the pit of her stomach, but now she looked up defiantly. At once her center of gravity plummeted into its right spot; her body responded to his over the three feet between them.

"Ay, ay, ay como riega los claveles
Ay, ay, ay que floriditos los tienes!"

He had left the first verse behind, changing the steps and snapping his fingers in more intricate rhythms. She followed with growing, exhilarated confidence. Now and then he would interrupt himself to show her a figure. It did not break the spell.

"Sol y luna, luna y cielo
Donde estuviste a noche . . ."

"Here comes the turn! Three times now!"

She drilled her toe into the floor the way he had shown her, a step that allowed her to spin around with ease, once, twice — A pain, sharp and mean, stabbed through her unshod foot.

"Ay, ay, ay como riega los claveles . . ."

With a splinter sticking in her toe, she stumbled. He caught her and swept her into his arms.

The world sank away.

* * *

They did not hear the approaching footsteps nor the squeaking of the latch. It took some vigorous throat-clearing from the newcomers to startle the pair back into an unkind reality.

Bartholomaeus stood on the threshold, accompanied by Antonio Giunta.

" 'And in the book that day we read no further,' " the Italian quoted.

Vrone managed to shoot him a withering look before, at a glance from her father, she walked out of the room, the splinter in her toe driving itself deeper into the flesh with every step. Yet there was no limp in her gait.

Bartholomaeus eyed Miguel with weary annoyance. His second marriage had left him with a loathing for scenes, but one seemed imminent, and he was obviously expected to play the role of the outraged father.

Miguel did not wait for the first thunderclap. He knew his duty. Why wait until the old man reminded him of it?

"Master Faber, I shall marry Veronica."

The words rang out, their echo hanging in the air like smoke after a pistol shot.

Unimpressed, Bartholomaeus went to one of the knocked-over chairs, righted it, and sat down. "This is a rather sudden move," he declared.

The young Spaniard frowned, irritated by this gratuitous statement. Why quibble over an act of necessity? Why was Faber not in a grateful hurry to call the girl and join their hands with his blessing? God knew that he, Miguel, was paying dearly but loyally for a moment of abandon. Farewell, Padua . . .

The printer leaned back in his chair and studied the ceiling for a while. Then his eyes met those of the young man.

"Miguel," he said, "had you asked me yesterday for Vrone's hand, it would have been an honor. Today your decision to marry her is a favor. We can do without favors."

Mortified, Miguel felt the blood rushing to his head and buzzing in his temples. If only the plank floor would open up and swallow him, but not before he had strangled this Giunta, who had tactfully gone over to the table and was now leafing through woodcuts of jonquils and lady's-slippers, without, however, losing any of Bartholomaeus' words.

"You are quite a *hidalgo*, Miguel," Faber went on, "strict and honorable, a man of chivalry."

Miguel did not know how long he could hold still under this dry mockery.

"However" — and Bartholomaeus suddenly sounded sad and serious — "you have not yet learned the difference between a gift and a sacrifice."

Miguel was learning it that very instant. "I shall go to Padua, Master Faber," he began, "and in two years I will have my degree — "

"In two years, Miguel," the printer interrupted him, "much water will have flown down the Rhine."

What did that mean? Did Faber want to prevent him from making idle promises? Was he saying that in two years things might look different? Was he allowing him to return, or was he intimating that in two years Mantua or Florence would be beckoning?

Giunta stirred. "I happen to be going back to Venice tonight," he said. "That is why I have come here, to take leave of my friends. There is a place in my coach. Signor de Roxas is welcome to it."

Miguel answered coldly, "Thank you. I shall find my way to Venice alone."

He bowed to the two men and was gone.

Faber gazed after him, half-angry, half-amused.

"He shall marry Veronica! Indeed! For a kiss, my heavens! Why, the boy truly thought he had put an indelible mark on the girl and deigned to offer marriage — the gall of it!"

"Were you not too hard on him?"

"No. He would have married Vrone out of a misguided sense of honor. My daughter deserves more than that. Mind you, he could not come from better stock: his father was a fine and honorable man. Let him run his head against a few walls. It will do him nothing but good."

"Well, young wine must storm and roar," Giunta observed indulgently.

"Quite so," Faber agreed, "but not in *my* cellar."

Miguel tore through his scanty belongings, packed a thin coat bag, and hurried down the wooden stairs.

Vrone stood on the landing. "What happened, Miguel? What happened?"

He could not trust himself to talk and could not muster the cruelty to pretend that he would be back. So he kissed her good-bye, a hasty, tormented kiss, and ran out of the house, through the narrow lanes where the wrought-iron tavern signs stuck out from the walls, vying for the traveler's attention, the Boar, the Lion, the Hedgehog. It was as if they wanted to hold him back, but he hurried toward the East Gate. Only when he was walking on the high road to Zürich did he take on a steadier pace.

A thin, drizzling rain had set in. Miguel almost welcomed it, for the moderate physical discomfort distracted him from a welter of confused feelings. Shame, he discovered, burned more viciously than grief. For a few steps he walked on, his eyes closed tightly, his hands over his ears, as if to shut out all shapes and voices that could lead his mind back to Faber's words: *We can do without favors.*

Had he really wanted to marry the girl? Certainly not, what with his plans for a career at the Gonzaga court! He had merely considered it his duty to declare himself ready to marry her, and had ended up being insulted by that conceited burgher. His conscience immediately protested against thinking of Faber in such ungrateful terms, but he silenced it.

The gray, misty air suddenly took on color before his eyes. He saw himself sitting with the Duke of Mantua at an exquisitely decked dinner table, all silver, crystal, and majolica, discussing some scientific problem with the enlightened ruler. Then he stood at the sickbed of the lovely duchess, curing her of a disease hitherto fatal . . .

The rain, mixed with half-melted snowflakes, blotted out the imagery.

Wheels turning and sloshing in the mud rolled nearer and nearer, and a carriage drew up beside him. Antonio Giunta stuck out his head and called to him, "Signor de Roxas, may I repeat my invitation to you to join me on my journey?"

Miguel stood beside the coach. I'd rather drown, he was about to say. The rain was pouring down, but his pride prevented him from accepting Giunta's offer. His pride? Wasn't it his pride that had landed him on this sodden road, drenched and shivering, sick with mortification? To hell with it.

He climbed in.

Vrone sat on her bed. One black stocking was lying on the wooden floor. She held her bare left foot across her right knee, intent on pulling the splinter out of the toe. Blinded by tears, she was having no easy time of it. The chip was deeply embedded in the flesh, and her fingernails were short. It took much tugging and squeezing before it came out. The pain was sharp, but it distracted her for an instant from her heart's distress. She held the splinter between thumb and forefinger. It was nearly an inch long, rough and bloody.

She rose, hobbled over to her oak chest, opened it, and rummaged among her linens until she found what she was looking for: a white lace handkerchief. She wrapped the splinter in it and laid the little bundle on the bottom of the chest, between two fragrant pomanders. Then she closed the heavy lid.

Rain was drumming against her window, soft and desolate, the water streaking down the green and red glass roundels. Evening came, blotting out their gentle glow, and turned into night.

Her tears had run dry. Slowly she undressed and went to bed, but sleep would not come. With burning eyes she looked into the darkness, waiting for the bleak morning.

he welcome was tumultuous. Laughing, Miguel freed himself from the embraces and questions of a dozen greeters, among them Vitus, Spina, Bayard, and Mirella, the buxom hostess of the Ox.

"Later," he said when pressed for an account of his whereabouts, and sat down.

Vitus called for wine. Mirella brought not only a full pitcher, but also a plateful of squid fried in olive oil and blessed with garlic, accompanied by a staff of golden wheat bread. Miguel's nostrils flared with recognition and pleasure. He closed his eyes for an instant, almost convinced that he had never been gone. The travails and travels of the last months fading away, he was aware of his absence only insofar as his friends were bringing him up to date on local events.

The new anatomy theater was finished; it would hold six hundred spectators. Acqua's assistant had been fired: the young man's scientific curiosity had been his undoing. With unseemly eagerness, he had seized the still-beating heart of a delinquent who had been quartered alive. The man in question, convicted for the murder of a noblewoman, had all the same been a Gritti, and the family had complained to the Venetian Senate. Acquapendente had been furious, but now he might console himself, Spina remarked good-naturedly, since Miguel de Roxas, his "favorite son," was back and could easily step into that bungler's shoes. Angiolina had married, yes, an innkeeper, but still welcomed the visits of former friends whenever her husband was off to the fish market in Chioggia.

To his surprise, Miguel received this last piece of news with equanimity.

Then he was called on to satisfy his companions' curiosity about his own adventures, but they had to content themselves with a short and cautious report. Vitus did not ask for details; he knew that Miguel would not withhold them once they could talk in private.

After some more drinking and joking, Miguel planted two kisses on Mirella's fire-reddened cheeks and left with Vitus.

The latter's assets had increased. The Bishop of Brixen had shown interest in the young student his village priest had spoken of with much praise. Vitus now received a small stipend that allowed him to devote more time to his studies and to rent a lean-to from a particularly stingy widow. Miguel accepted his friend's hospitality for the night. The next morning he looked for quarters of his own.

The journey with Giunta had yielded unexpected possibilities. The Venetian printer, after mellowing his passenger's ferocious mood with a few witty, friendly words and winning him over with his civility, had proposed that Miguel work for him as a corrector.

"Bartholomaeus praised you to the skies," he had said. "I should feel fortunate to assure the Giunta Press of your services."

They had agreed that Miguel would divide his time

166

between his studies and his work at the printshop. It was now mid-April, and there would be time enough for the young man to audit lectures and to prepare himself for the fall term while earning his keep.

It was a busy summer. Sometimes Miguel would take the boat to Venice as often as three times a week to work on Giunta's books. The printer occupied a house on a narrow canal where Venice's artists and scholars frequently convened, sometimes accompanied by their very literate mistresses, who were kind indeed to the handsome young Spaniard.

Now and then a volume from the Faber Press would arrive at the Giunta shop, bearing the firm's sign on the title page, a hammer and anvil with a sunburst of sparks. *Anno Domini MDLXXXI, apud Veronicam, B. Fabri filiam*, Miguel would read. It always gave him a sense of urgency, of an option still open, and of possible later regret, but the feeling was so scant, so fleeting, that he could easily dismiss it. Besides, he was too busy, working overtime for his tuition and also for a new wardrobe, for Giunta had promised him that he would present him to Messer Giovanni Tiepolo, the Republic's ambassador at the Gonzaga court.

The months passed swiftly; summer turned into fall. The Bora threw the waves high up on Saint George's column, and a damp chill rose from the canals.

On the nineteenth of October, Saint Luke's Day, the new term at the university was solemnly opened with a convocation of faculty, students, clergy, and town officials, as well as two representatives of the Venetian Senate.

Miguel de Roxas, duly matriculated, walked in the procession.

* * *

167

The fire in the emblazoned hearth burned off only the worst edge of the Castilian winter day. The cardinal sat in an armchair, close to the crackling logs.

Padre Domingo was seated somewhat farther away from the source of heat, since the layer of fat around his short frame kept him sufficiently comfortable.

"Continue, Vega," the cardinal said to his secretary, who stood before him, reciting the day's dispatches. Don Pedro's eyes had become too weak to read even the careful calligraphy of chancellery scribes.

. . . the anatomy was conducted by Professor Acquapendente, assisted most ably by Max Cresser of Nürnberg and Miguel de Roxas of Saragossa.

Since Your Eminence has enjoined me by letter of November 30, A.D. *1580, to be on the alert for the latter-mentioned to reappear at Padua's university, I therefore respectfully submit the above report, awaiting Your Eminence's orders.*

I kiss Your Eminence's hands in utter devotion.

Your Eminence's humble servant

At Venice,
this thirtieth of October
Anno a Virginis partu
MDLXXXI

Francisco de Garcíhernandez
His Catholic Majesty's Ambassador
to the Republic of St. Mark.

The cardinal straightened up against the back of his chair. The ghost of a smile played around the corners of his mouth. "Are the messengers ready?"

"Yes, Your Eminence."

Vega installed himself at a little table, dipped his quill into the inkwell, and held it poised over a sheet of paper.

"To Garcíhernandez," the cardinal dictated. "Miguel de Roxas is to pursue his studies undisturbed but closely watched. As soon as the degree of *doctor medicinae* is conferred upon him, you are to ensure yourself of his live person and have him brought to Toledo."

Padre Domingo concealed his shock under a placid mien. The news of Miguel de Roxas' survival was unsettling enough, but the cardinal's response to it enraged him. He had understood at once why the young man was allowed the time to finish his studies in Italy: no Spanish university could have given him the training available at Padua's School of Medicine. So the cardinal had not given up his plans for the young man; indeed, still considered him fit for royal service, a twice-disobedient miscreant suspected of murder, and the son of a convicted heretic, who would look much better in a penitent's shirt and dunce cap one fine afternoon in the Plaza Mayor than in a doctor's gown at the bedside of the king! How long would it take Miguel de Roxas to fulfill his academic requirements? Two years? Without altering his friendly gaze, the padre observed the cardinal's gaunt and weakened features. Hippocratic lines? No. Not quite yet, he decided, but the next two years could bring changes and chances. Now was the time for waiting.

Gil de Vega desired Miguel de Roxas' death for more mundane reasons. Still, he too understood that the watchword was patience. Confidently, he braced himself for the vigil. One look at the monk told him that the days of Miguel de Roxas and those of the cardinal were now being measured by the same hourglass.

n their business office Bartholomaeus Faber and his daughter sat over the firm's accounts, which showed a net profit of five thousand florins for the year 1580.

"Not bad, Vroneli," the printer declared, hoping to coax a smile from her. She remained impassive, and he looked at her with concern. The gray light of a cloudy day falling through the window's clear glass roundels did nothing to soften the lines of her face, grown thin and haggard.

The day after Miguel left she had appeared at the printshop at the usual hour and gone about her business as if nothing had happened. This went on for weeks, and Faber was beginning to hope that in due time the young Spaniard's image would cease to haunt his daughter's thoughts. Miguel had not written after his hasty departure, and, in a way, Faber had welcomed this show of ingratitude, believing that indignation over such behavior would speed Vrone's recovery.

The other day, however, a pack of books had arrived at the shop. Luckily, the printer himself received the consignment — Giunta's new edition of the *Aeneid* in four volumes, accompanied by a letter from Miguel de Roxas to Bartholomaeus Faber and his daughter, a letter of thanks and apology. Bartholomaeus had managed to hide it in his sleeve before Vrone entered; she would have recognized the straight Spanish hand above the broken seal.

Ignoring a few pangs of his conscience — after all, the letter was addressed to Vrone as well as to himself — Faber had decided that there was no reason to tamper with a healing wound. But was it healing?

Had he been too rash? Would he have brushed aside Miguel's admittedly arrogant proposal if he could have foreseen his daughter's distress? It was too late now. The letter from Venice, though respectful, did not repeat the offer.

He would take Vrone on a journey, he thought. She needed a change of sky. To Venice, perhaps — to Amsterdam, he angrily corrected himself.

* * *

By virtue of the power conferred on the Faculty of this University by the Serenissime Republic of Venice and by the Worthy Town of Padua we bestow upon thee, Michael de Roxas, the title of Doctor Medicinae, with its perquisites and privileges, and, in view of thine exemplary diligence and ability, summa cum laude.

Given in the Good Town of
Padua this 24th of August
Anno Domini MDLXXXI

Miguel took the scroll from the rector's hand. It was now his turn to thank the venerable faculty and to make a speech in praise of Medicine. His address was brief, the ceremony in the great hall already having lasted for seven hours.

Released at last, the new doctors hurried to their respective quarters to shed their long robes and put away their hard-earned sheepskins before gathering again for the graduation banquet at the Ox.

Mirella was outdoing herself. Over a blazing fire, seven lambs were turning on the spits. Huge bowls of lettuce, fennel, cucumbers, and shiny black olives, plates heaped with oil-fried fish and prawns, were awaiting the hungry scholars. Their thirst would be quenched by the region's red wine decanted from straw-clad bottles.

They took over the place "like the Gauls the Capitol," according to the host, who over the years had acquired a smattering of classical allusions from his clientele.

At the head table Miguel and Vitus were surrounded by well-wishers. They were the only ones to be leaving Padua the following morning. Vitus had received his degree merely *cum laude*, but this, he said, would sufficiently impress his sponsor, the Bishop of Brixen, who had offered him a place among his physicians, thus increasing their number to four.

"Thank God for the old hypochondriac." He laughed. "Now I can marry Cilli and hang out my shingle."

Whenever Vitus talked about his plans, Miguel felt a little superior, considering his friend's modest prospects. It was true that Vitus' folk were peasants and that had it not been for the local priest, who had singled out the bright boy and taught him Latin, today there would be no Vitus Tracterus Scalericus, Doctor Medicinae Universitatis Patavii. Everybody in the village of Schallern had contributed to sending Vitus to Padua, even the gravedigger, who could neither read nor write. Miguel liked to imagine the new doctor's return to his hamlet, as he displayed his scroll and made all those good people feel that they, too, had a part in this glory.

As for himself, thanks to Giunta's patient and clever mediation he was expecting a loftier career. At nine in the morning the Gonzaga carriage would halt in front of the cathedral and bring him to Mantua, where he would take up his duties as physician to the duke's children.

It was way after midnight when the party began to disband. The farewells took a long time, as did the many kisses bestowed on Mirella and her flushed helpmates, but at last the young men stepped out of the stuffy tavern into the cool, pure night. Vitus, who had abandoned his cramped quarters and rapacious landlady for the newly appreciated Bursa, was walking Miguel home. They strolled over the silent square of Saint Anthony, past the pedestal of Donatello's horseman, troubled by an unadmitted sadness at the inevitable parting. Miguel suspected his friend of fighting back tears. "Remember Spina?" he asked quickly.

They laughed. Spina, drunk, had accepted a bet to climb the pedestal and mount Gattamelata's horse; a dozen students challenged him at five scudi apiece. He had managed it, but the descent proved difficult. His colleagues, after applauding the feat, were reluctant to pay up. They had left him sitting on his high horse and, ignoring his cries, had gone home. The morning found him sober, terrified, and holding on to the horse's neck — until the Town Guards had hauled him down.

The two had almost arrived at Miguel's quarters in the narrow Via del Bove, when Vitus stopped in his tracks. "Look."

Near the door there were two shadows, barely moving.

"I don't like it," the Tyrolean said. "Come, walk me home. Let's go to the Bursa."

The Spanish Embassy in Venice had a few reliable professionals at its beck and call for transporting recalcitrant subjects of His Catholic Majesty back into the kingdom or dispatching them altogether. The present assignment, however, was unpleasant to the experts in charge because of contradictory orders.

A "live person" had to be brought from Padua aboard the galleon *La Soltera* moored at the harbor and bound for Valencia — mere child's play. What disturbed them were half-spoken and quickly recanted intimations that in certain quarters the news of the "live person's" demise would be welcome and amply rewarded. Yet this counterorder, they understood, depended on the state of health of the cardinal. The stronger he was, the more desirable the "person's" decease. On the other hand, a sufficiently recovered cardinal would have a long arm, long enough to reach those guilty of such an act of blatant disobedience.

It was decided to carry out the assignment step by step, allowing for the interference of chance.

A few goldpieces had changed hands during the last weeks. They had purchased information concerning the hours of the graduation banquet and of Roxas' planned departure for Mantua. Six Spaniards had come to Padua aboard a barge that was now moored near the bridge gate.

The two young men arrived at the Bursa, where much drinking and singing was still going on. Toward three in the morning Miguel decided to go back to his quarters.

"Let me come with you," Vitus proposed. "I want to be sure that the coast is clear. They've left you alone a little too long."

Again they walked across the deserted church square, through dark alleys.

Suddenly Miguel felt an arm across his throat, pulling him backward; then it slackened. Vitus had drawn his dagger and stabbed Miguel's aggressor, but the man, though mortally wounded, still had the strength to run his knife into Vitus' chest before he collapsed. A second Spaniard fell over Miguel, but was silenced by a dirk-thrust in the throat. Miguel knelt by Vitus, whose mouth was gushing blood.

"Run — " he gasped. "The canal . . ."

Miguel shook his head and began cutting open his friend's doublet.

"Run . . . you ass! Don't let it . . . be for nothing . . ."

He ran. In long, loping strides, darting in and out of the narrow lanes, he neared the canal. There — the wall gate, the bridge — but there stood another soldier. Miguel turned to the right and hurried on, grazing the wall. At the next bridge three men were waiting for him. They overcame him and dragged him toward the barge. Miguel let himself go limp, biding his time. As soon as he was on the boat's deck, he tore loose from his surprised captors and plunged overboard. The water closed over him.

The three drew their pistols and emptied them into the river. Swimming low and diving as often as he could, Miguel could feel the bullets hit the water left and right. He kept even with the current, praying that he would not end up in a mill race — the river was turning quite a few wheels — and striving for the left bank. Luckily he had not worn his boots to the banquet, but his Florentine suede slippers. His close-fitting doublet, breeches, and hose, though soaked, did not weigh him down too much, yet still hampered his movements. At last he reached the muddy edge, pulled himself ashore, and fell exhausted into the rushes.

Clouds had been covering the stars; now it began to rain. Miguel slid deeper into the grass, pressing himself against the swampy ground. He saw the barge glide by, slowly, deliberately. The men searched the river with torches, but the black waters did not yield their secret.

Fear shook him. Why did they want to bring him back to Spain? To punish him for his disobedience, he was sure. The stake was awaiting him. He would kill himself ten times before they had a chance to drag him up to the wood-pile — he would not end like Servetus. But he was not dying; not yet. Painfully he rose and waded deeper into the swamp. The soil gave way; he sank in to his knees. This would never do, he saw. He went down flat on his stomach and dragged himself ahead. Like a worm, he thought.

Aboard the barge the three held a war council. They were almost sure that their quarry had drowned, but to be on the safe side, they would get some horses in the morning and check the road northward along the Brenta.

The swamp emptied into a rice field. It was a gloomy morning, hot and muggy. A million crickets were whirring. It was as if the heat itself had a voice that grew louder the higher the sun climbed behind the gray clouds.

Miguel rose to get his bearings. Rice fields on all sides.

Half a mile to his left, he suspected, lay the Brenta and the road. He began to wade again, each step making a gurgling noise as he pulled his foot out of the soaked ground. His clothes were still wet and steaming. He took off his doublet and shirt. The first, he rolled around his waist by knotting the sleeves together; the shirt he wore as a twisted kerchief against the veiled but vicious sun rays.

There was not a soul around, but he kept ducking every five or six steps. After he had spent hours in wading and crawling, a house with a long brick roof came into sight. He straightened, looked around, and at once dived among the rice stalks: far away, in the heat-glimmering distance, he had spotted a dust cloud on the road, stirred up by a couple of riders. He made it to the end of the field, gained the narrow trail, and reached the house.

The door stood ajar. In the sooty kitchen sat an old woman, surrounded by a few children in tatters. She had the youngest one on her lap and was allowing it to suck her dirty finger.

Miguel staggered in.

The old woman looked at him with the cunning smile of the insane. "Spaniards after you?" she asked.

"Yes." He had no time to be surprised by her guess.

She rose and put the baby on the dirt floor, where it started to scream.

"This time I'll be more clever; they won't cut off your ears and your nose . . . Del Vasto's after you? Oh, he is a bad one . . . Get in here."

She pushed him into a windowless room and pointed to a heap of straw, covered with a sack that must once have been a featherbed. "Lie down here."

He obeyed. She covered him with the reeking rag.

The three Spaniards were riding on the dusty road, a causeway along the Brenta through the rice fields. They had searched the few scattered hovels, thoroughly frightening man and beast, but had found nothing. Now they came to the house where Miguel had found shelter.

The old woman had found her seat in the kitchen again and put her finger into the baby's mouth, as before.

"Seen anyone running north, mother?" one of the riders asked. After six months in Venice he had acquired some Italian.

"Not I, my handsome gentleman, not I," she wheezed, "but if you don't believe me, why don't you look? The man and his woman are in the fields," she added.

The three walked through the house, an act quickly done. "You haven't seen my bedroom, gentlemen," she reminded them. "Who wants to see your chaste bed, old witch?" their spokesman said; and to the others: "Nothing here. He must already be farther north."

They left.

She went back to Miguel and pulled the rag off him.

"They are gone, son. But don't you stir. They'll be back. Lie still."

He lay motionless, spent, under the foul cloth, sick at the loathsome familiarity of it all. Again he was fleeing, the Holy Office at his heels. The first time he had left a dead scoundrel in his tracks, but this time he had abandoned his dying friend.

Don't let it be for nothing. He had made good his escape, hadn't he? He was now being protected by a madwoman . . . A fit of laughter shook him. It ended in a dry sob.

The woman rushed in. "Quiet, son, for the sake of Jesus! They might be back."

His fear flared up again. If they came back, he would have to kill himself. He felt for his dagger and closed his fingers around its hilt. A terrible regret seized him, nameless and formless at first, but quickly taking shape. It was Vrone's face he saw. What a fool he had been! Mantua, the Gonzagas, indeed! Why hadn't he written to her? He had done so, to be sure. A coldly impeccable letter had gone off to Basel, the thought of which now made him wince. Would she ever forgive him? Would he ever have the chance to ask her forgiveness? He started. He was still alive. Why did he dream of dying? Luck, in the shape of a demented crone, had outwitted his pursuers so far. Let her but keep them farther off his path and he would make it back to Basel, he vowed, on his knees, if must be.

He slid deeper under the rag, as if to make himself all but invisible.

"Clever darling!" The woman had reappeared, with a bundle of clothes under her arm.

"They are for you. But wait a spell. Vasto is a bad one. They still may come by again. Mayn't they?"

She turned toward a corner, and Miguel saw that she was speaking to someone there. Straining his eyes in the darkness, he saw a creature squatting on the floor, as wizened as his rescuer. It was — or had been — a man. There was no nose in his face, not even a hole. The flesh had somehow grown together over the wound. He was breathing through his mouth.

Miguel de Roxas, *doctor medicinae* and anatomist, averted his eyes. Then he forced himself to look at the luckless being. What had happened? And what was the name the old woman kept repeating? Vasto . . . del Vasto . . . del Vasto, one of the Imperial generals at Pavia! The name was still famous, although its bearer had been dead for many a year. Now he easily pieced together the story. The man in the corner probably had fallen victim to the marauding troops that swarmed all over Lombardy in the days of the great battle. He and his wife must have been barely in their twenties then. The woman probably had never recovered from the shock. Miguel looked at her with awe. Her fear, undying, had saved his own life, sixty years later.

She had gone outside and now came back.

"They're riding northward," she said and pointed to the bundle.

In the evening the farmer and his wife trudged in from the fields. They confirmed their guest's conjecture about the old man.

"They cut off his nose and his ears because he would not give up his wedding ring. Why, he was lucky they did not cut off anything else! The old mother has been crazy ever since."

The family was sheltering Miguel the way the Italian peasant, from time immemorial, had sheltered fugitives from both the spiritual and secular arms. At the same time, they had one of their children sitting in the rice field to spy on the Spanish horsemen, realistically assessing the conditions under which they could send their guest on his way again.

Miguel now shared the life of Lombardian rice farmers. After three or four days he began to go out into the fields, taking part in their backbreaking work to earn his keep. Within a short time no one could have recognized the would-be court physician in the dirty, stubble-bearded peasant.

Again, he was on his way to Basel, pursued by the Holy Office, but this time there was an urgency in his heart that made him chafe even at the delay he had to observe for his safety. *What if she had married in the meantime?* He wished that his eyes could see through mountains, over valleys, into the ink-smudged workshop!

Day after muggy day passed, until at last one of the children came running: the Spaniards were riding south again. Indeed, they could be seen in the distance, passing on the road and disappearing beneath the gray-white horizon.

Miguel took leave of his hosts. The younger woman had washed his clothes; they looked considerably worse for wear, but suited a poor vagrant scholar.

The farmer led him to the road. "Follow the Brenta," he said, "and go with God."

Follow the Brenta — follow the Gallego — How far to the mountains?

Emaciated, almost spectral, the cardinal was leaning against heaped pillows.

"Has the body been found?" he asked.

"No, Your Eminence. Miguel de Roxas was shot while swimming the Brenta Canal. He drowned."

Was it true? Gil de Vega asked himself. As long as he did not see Miguel de Roxas' dead body stretched out at his feet, he could not quiet the whispering voice of doubt.

"He drowned, Your Eminence," he repeated. "There were witnesses."

The cardinal did not answer. He had closed his eyes. Suddenly his mind, like the flame of a dying candle, erupted in a flare of light. He guessed — no, he knew — that Miguel was alive.

I am not worth it, my God, he thought, but his blood is not on my head.

The smile did not reach his lips, for the bullet had finally reached his heart.

arefully, Miguel walked on, looking over his shoulder every few yards, ready to duck into the rice fields at the sight of the smallest dust cloud in the road. He spent the night under a tree and was on his feet again at sunrise. After a while a carter appeared. Miguel, having watched him approach and judging him safe, asked to be taken up and was given a ride as far as Bassano, where they arrived late in the afternoon.

After Bassano the road turned sharply westward, mounting between orchards and vineyards, which were peopled with harvesters. Three years had passed since he trod the grapes in the Garonne Valley on his flight from Spain. Again he offered his help in return for food and shelter and was willingly accepted. He would stay for a day or two, climbing pear trees or cutting grapes, then go on his way until he had eaten up the earned provisions. After a week he reached Trient and the mountains. Unlike the white and gray rocks of the Pyrenees, the immense crags here were red, as were the stones of the town's crenelated walls. He saw it all in the light of a luminous fall day and would have marveled at the sight, had he not been so impatient to press on.

With every mile gained, he felt safer. Those fleeing

from King Philip's Inquisition had little to fear in Austria. Emperor Rudolf detested his uncle and, far from shipping back the refugees to Spain, offered them sanctuary.

"There is only one road to Switzerland," the guardian of Meran's Franciscan monastery explained to Miguel, who had spent a night in one of the guest cells. "It leads through the Münster Valley to Zernez. It begins at Schlanders, and then you can go either by Prad or by Schallern."

Miguel's heart froze.

It was more than five weeks since Vitus' death. They must have learned about it by now, he thought. Learned about it? How? A letter from Padua up to those mountains easily took two months or longer.

During the first days of his flight, in the rice farmer's house, Miguel had thought about Vitus only once; then his mind stopped short of recollecting the events of that last night in Padua. The will to survive had pushed aside the image of Vitus bleeding to death in the dark alley. He had not even wondered about who might have found him in the morning.

The river in the narrow valley fell foaming over blocks of granite. The road was mounting. A farmer driving an ox cart caught up with the solitary wanderer and offered to take him up to Prad. Miguel accepted with a sigh of relief. Providence had spared him a decision. Was he not in a hurry? The cart rumbled on. His companion, who had not spoken three words during the last hour, indicated a squat granite church tower about a mile away.

"There is Prad," he said. Miguel climbed down from the crossboard.

"And where is Schallern?" he heard himself say.

The man pointed back over his shoulder.

"You should have told me before," he said, flicked the ox with his stick, and took a small side path that presumably led to his farm.

Miguel began walking straight ahead. His mind was blank, but he felt that he was now wearing boots of lead. Slowly he came to a halt. For a while he stood still, looking into the valley, his hair tousled by the mountain wind. Then he turned around.

The Reverend Radurner was puttering around his bee-hives, preparing them for the winter. He had just checked the flight holes, making sure that they were snugly waxed shut, when old Faustina, hastening over the broken garden steps, announced that a young man from Padua wanted to see him. From Padua! One of Vitus' colleagues, then? He felt pleased to have the chance, in his isolation, for a good talk with a man of learning.

When he entered the little refectory, one look at the visitor's face told him the young man had come with a different purpose. He took Miguel's hands in his and merely asked, "How?"

They sat down, and Miguel told the priest about the events on graduation night.

"God bless you," Radurner said. "You are a brave soul. You could have by-passed us" — Miguel felt the blood rush into his cheeks — "and we should have never known how he met his end. But we are not done. We must go and tell them." He seemed not to notice the pain and pleading in Miguel's eyes. "We will go up there in half an hour. Meanwhile you must eat something. I don't think you have eaten for quite a while," he added gently. "You will need your strength."

Faustina brought black bread, a jug of milk, and a comb of the priest's honey. Miguel, relieved of his burden, suddenly felt ravenous. He had barely finished his meal when the priest said, "Let us go now."

He led the way. Leaving the village, the two men climbed up a slope on which were scattered some lonely farmhouses, each surrounded by a few slanted acres of stony sod.

The Trachter house was the last one, standing just at the rim of the pine forest. It was built of rough granite blocks and had an overhanging, wood-shingled roof. The windows, small, squarish, and deep-set, held pots of red-flowering begonias, though the hazel bushes nearby had only some yellow leaves left.

A few chickens fluttered around. A dog, chained to its hut, barked shortly, then, having recognized the priest, settled down again to doze.

They entered.

The family was at supper. Sitting around the table, which occupied a quarter of the low-ceilinged kitchen, Blasius Trachter, his two sons, and three daughters were dipping their wooden spoons into a bowl of thick cabbage soup. On the table there was also a loaf of bread the size of a cartwheel, a mound of butter, and a jug of cider, which went from mouth to mouth.

Hardly a word was spoken while the spoons were working. The mother stood by the hearth, stirring the remainder of the soup in the kettle suspended on an iron chain over the fire.

Miguel stopped at the door. Unnoticed for a few moments, he looked at them. So these were Vitus' people, these angular, weather-beaten, silent folk.

Awkwardly and with much shuffling they rose at the sight of the priest.

"Praised be Jesus Christ," they greeted him.

"In all eternity, amen," he answered.

Meanwhile the mother had seen the unknown young man who was with Radurner. Her heart contracted. She leaned against the hearth wall, the spoon still in her hand.

Gently, the priest led her to the bench and made her sit down. "He is dead," she said.

Radurner nodded. "Yes, mother, he is dead."

She remained sitting upright, looking unseeingly ahead. The others stood benumbed.

Miguel waited for tears to flow the way one waits for a cloudburst after the lightning and the thunderclap. But their eyes stayed dry.

He had seen sorrowing souls at home as well as in Padua. There had always been weeping, wailing, and hand-wringing. It often seemed as if those mourners almost enjoyed their lamenting. The silent grief here bewildered him.

The priest brought him forward. Blasius Trachter invited him to sit down on the bench. One of the girls brought two wooden goblets and filled them with cider.

The Trachters posed no questions, but quietly waited for the newcomer to speak.

What was he to tell them? That their son had given his life to save him, a stranger who meant nothing to them? He pressed his lips together. Why had he poured out his tale to the priest? Would it not have been enough to bring the news of Vitus' death? Why should he have to face the unforgiving eyes of his friend's family?

He made it short. Vitus, he said, had been killed during an assault. The murderer's blade had gone through the lung. He had died on the spot.

Radurner translated. Then he said, "Tell them how Vitus happened to be in the street with you."

Miguel bowed his head. "You tell them, Reverend."

The priest spoke. It seemed to Miguel that the incomprehensible idiom of the mountain-dwellers was casting him out. He felt exposed and scorned.

The priest fell silent. Miguel forced himself to raise his head and meet the eyes of Vitus' mother. He saw bitterness there — and compassion.

Blasius asked a short question. Radurner turned to Miguel. "He wants to know where Vitus is buried."

The young man blanched. Buried? How was he to know? He had been told to run . . .

"You may lie," Radurner added quietly.

He might as well, Miguel thought. With luck, the Black Friars would have shoveled a grave in a corner of the Franciscans' churchyard; otherwise, the Spaniards may have thrown him into the canal. If the Town Guards found him, a poor foreign student, doctor or not, Vitus could well have made an appearance at the anatomy theater.

"He is buried in hallowed ground."

Wasn't this whole earth hallowed or cursed, depending on whether you believed that God or the Devil had made it?

Radurner rose. "We will now say a Paternoster for Vitus. Tomorrow we will have the Mass for him."

Night had fallen as the priest and Miguel began to

188

descend the trail into the valley. Moon and stars stood in the black, cloudless sky.

"You will sleep under my roof tonight," Radurner said, "and tomorrow, after Mass, you may go on your way."

At the presbytery they sat down to a meal of bread, butter, and fresh mushrooms. They ate in silence.

The priest let his clear, squinting eyes rest on his young guest for a while. "Don't be too proud in your grief, son," he said. "Vitus would have given his life for anyone in danger. Just see to it that he did not make too bad a bargain."

Requiem aeternam dona ei, Domine.

The church was filled to the last pew. They all had come to mourn Vitus' death, as they all had contributed to his brief career.

After the service the priest joined the Trachter family and beckoned Miguel to come near. "Wherever his body has found its rest," he said, "this was his burial. You have brought your friend home."

Vitus' mother came forward and gave Miguel a small book. It was Ovid's *Metamorphoses*, a gift from the Bishop of Brixen.

"It belonged to him," Radurner said. "She cannot read it and she wants you to have it."

Miguel looked into her careworn face.

"The Lord giveth, the Lord taketh away," she said slowly. "The Lord's name be praised."

The next day he was on his way. Radurner had given him a letter of recommendation for the Bishop of Chur.

"The road leads over Zernez," he said. "You should make it within two days. And now go with God."

He walked briskly, then turned his head to look back at Schallern. Once more he saw the stone houses in the steep, wooded valley and the squarish church tower with its round-arched bell window.

"The Lord giveth, the Lord taketh away." He taketh away, indeed, Miguel thought. So why should the Lord's name be praised?

Two days later he reached Qernez. From there the way to Chur was long. The old coat Radurner had given him did not protect him from the cutting wind and the first snow flurries. His discomfort, however, ended when he arrived at the bishop's residence. Radurner's letter recommended him so warmly that His Episcopal Grace not only invited the young Spaniard for dinner; he ordered a carriage to take him to Zürich. Beyond Zürich, unfortunately, the bishop's jurisdiction and influence ended, so Miguel had to descend from the comfortable vehicle and continue his journey on foot.

Mile after mile he walked, until his sorely tried suede slippers nearly fell off his feet. He slept on straw in the stables of roadside inns and ate with carters and journeymen who would share a meal with him for splinting a fracture or pulling a tooth.

Every day he saw the roofs and spires of Basel on the horizon — and then one winter evening the thick, round wall towers rose before his unbelieving eyes.

He called out his name to the guard, who, half asleep, merely mumbled, "Pass." Hurrying through the Crooked

Lane, past the Boar and the Hedgehog, he reached the moon-lit little square.

He gathered a few pebbles and pitched them one by one against Vrone's window.

Having sat up with her father to discuss the firm's next project, a new edition of Copernicus' works, Vrone had gone to bed later than usual. Now she was sleeping under her red-checkered, down-filled comforter, with Lucifer curled up at her feet.

"You're getting on, Vrone," Babeli had observed recently. "It looks as if that cat may be all you'll ever have to share your bed with."

"That suits me fine," the girl had replied. "He keeps my feet warm."

And he won't ever break your heart, Babeli had been about to add, but she thought better of it.

Vrone had never mentioned Miguel again, thus silently asking the old woman to do likewise. Still, it hurt Babeli not to voice her indignation and sorrow at watching the girl turn into an old maid before her very eyes.

Her face pale and drawn, Vrone would come and go between the house and the shop. Indeed, she had never worked more assiduously. Book after book left the Faber Press, works of ancient and contemporary authors, each one exquisitely printed, and the old texts annotated by distinguished scholars. Nor were calendars and cookbooks neglected.

Bartholomaeus, though proud of his daughter, had begun to be frightened by her joyless diligence. When not at the shop, she would stay home. At the most, on sunny days she would sit in the garden or take a walk with her father. Twice Shrove Tuesday had come and gone. Twice she had declined invitations to the yearly evening dance at Town Hall. There were parties and festive target-shooting matches on the Rhine field. Vrone was not seen there anymore, she who often had quietly put on her spectacles and hit the bull's eye, to the delighted applause of the men from the Sharpshooter's Guild.

Would she ever forget that foreigner? Babeli kept wondering. What was wrong with the home-grown fellows? The Frobens, the Platters, the Isingrins? Well, their looks, for one thing, the old woman had to admit. Some of them might cut a reasonably fine figure, but none could hold a candle to that tall, slim devil with his dark hair and deep blue eyes. Yes, he had been a pleasure to behold, but this alone, Babeli knew, would not have won him Vrone's heart.

Often, she remembered, when assignments were pressing, the girl would have her bring some food to the shop at midday. There, the two young people would be sitting at opposite ends of the great table, working away at the mass of proof sheets and notes, and exchanging low-voiced comments in Italian. Sometimes they would laugh, softly and mischievously. As soon as they saw her, they would push aside the papers to make room for two plates and two goblets and eat in cheerful disorder. Babeli, ignorant of the language and thus not distracted by the meaning of their talk, would feel all the more keenly the subtle bliss and brightness that reigned in the untidy shop.

Those two may have been meant for each other, she mused. She was certain that Vrone knew it, but the Spaniard, true man that he was, conceited and slow-witted, had not grasped it and never would. Otherwise, he would have come back.

Saint Catherine struck eleven. Vrone, vaguely aware of it, was turning a little under her featherbed when she heard a pebble strike her window. I bet it's Ruedi, she thought drowsily. The Widow Brechbühler's new husband — they lived next door — sometimes was too drunk to hit the right house, let alone the right window, whenever he came home without his key. She waited for the creaking of the Brechbühlers' house gate and for the widow's tearful remonstrances. Everything was still.

Another little stone, aimed with precision, bounced off the glass-pane's lead-framed rounds.

Vrone jumped out of bed and opened the window. There stood a man — a vagrant, as far as she could make out in the uncertain moonlight.

"Move on!" she called down to him.

But he stepped nearer until he stood straight under her window.

"Move on," she repeated. "D'you want the slopjar on your head?"

He did not stir. "Veronica," he whispered.

She gasped. Her hand went to her heart.

"Veronica — " She did not even hear him. Leaving the window pane flapping in the cold breeze, barefoot, in her nightgown, she raced down the wooden stairs, with trembling hands pulled back the bolt, opened the door on the bedraggled traveler, and threw herself into his arms.

heet Three, Chapter Seventeen continued. Go on, Martin."

"*A prince should make himself feared in such a way*," the lad read in a mountain-dweller's heavily accented Latin, "*that if he gets no love, he gets no hate either, because it is perfectly possible to be feared and not hated.*"

A little smugly, Vrone nodded assent. She ran her print-shop somewhat according to those precepts. Sound fellow, Machiavelli, she thought.

"*This will be the result if the prince will keep his hands off the property of his subjects and off their women . . .* Mistress Vrone, I understand the part about the women, but must not a prince tax his subjects?"

Vrone rolled her eyes heavenward. "Martin," she said with a sigh, "don't *read* the stuff! We are collating. I'll save you a copy."

"Why, thank you, Mistress Vrone."

She grimaced a little. A year before, Miguel had traveled to Schallern and offered to sponsor Vitus' younger brother through a curriculum at Padua. Blasius Trachter would have accepted gladly, but his wife would not hear of it. Vitus' death had left her with a dread of that town. Instead,

Martin Trachter had become a printer's apprentice in Basel.

He was bright, eager to learn, and in awe of Vrone. Sometimes, though, during proofreading, he would try her patience by getting lost in thought over some pregnant sentence instead of combing the text for misprints. On the other hand, he was trustworthy and thus privy to her business venture of reprinting the Latin version of the famous and infamous political primer, for which she anticipated brisk sales.

"Go on, Martin."

"But when the Prince has to shed blood he should not touch the victim's estate, for men will be quicker to forget the death of a father than the loss of an inheritance ..."

Vrone whistled through her teeth. The sound seemed to come from the lips of a street urchin rather than from those of Mistress Veronica de Roxas, *nata* Faber, proprietress and head of Basel's most prestigious printing firm.

So this is where the cardinal had gone for advice! *For men will be quicker to forget the death of a father than the loss of an inheritance ...* Wait till Miguel saw this!

Galley proof in hand, she was about to run out of the shop, across the street, and into his study, when she paused. Reading that passage, would he be as pleased as she was? Wouldn't it merely remind him of his life's worst moments? No, she would not show it to him. What if he should come upon it himself? Unlikely, she thought. All Miguel was reading these days were medical books, while cutting up countless rats in his "experiment shed" to find out which way the blood was running in the veins. She could safely keep her discovery for herself. It was to be her secret treasure, her talisman, this knowledge that Miguel had foiled the cardinal.

She sat and dreamed. It was now three years since the night pebbles had bounced off her window's bull's-eye glass. She thought back, reliving the endless embrace in the dark hall; remembering how perplexed and pleased Bartholomaeus had been, he who was now in his grave; how she and Miguel had been married; how little Juan was born; and how Miguel had set up his practice.

It had been an uphill fight. Basel's notables were shocked to see their favorite candidate for spinsterhood suddenly wed a foreigner — and a Papist to boot! (The Fabers, too, were Catholics, but all the same, they were Baslers!) It had taken Miguel the better part of two years to earn the townspeople's trust by his medical skill and his devotion to his patients. You could ask him to a sickbed in the dead of the night. (Old Dr. Veggli would pull the bedcovers over his head whenever called after midnight, telling frantic folk that an ill person either died at dawn or lived to see the next sun, so it made no sense to wake up a doctor.)

Miguel had not only done well by the citizenry; the past year the rector of the university, a Paduan alumnus, had invited him to deliver a few anatomy lectures, which were so successful that he was to repeat them the next term.

They kept a hospitable home, a trysting place for writers, artists, and scholars. Only the past week there had been a small dinner party to celebrate the Faber press's new edition of Copernicus' works. The visiting Giunta, fired by several glasses of Rhine wine, had improvised a hymn on the marriage of Aesculapius, the god of Medicine, with Urania, the muse of Astronomy.

Vrone smiled. A fig for the house in Saragossa and another one for the orchard! Besides, if *The Prince* sold half as well as she expected the book to do, they just might buy that vineyard on the Rhine . . .

"Mistress Vrone . . ."

She turned to her startled apprentice. "Forgive me, Martin," she said gently. "I was reading."

il de Vega, Count of Fuentes, felt sick. Chills ran down his spine. His head ached. To make things worse, he was lying in a strange bed, unattended. The Twelve Apostles Inn certainly was not living up to its reputation as one of Basel's finest hostelries. To be sure, he was lodged in the best room, but the servant girl had fled in superstitious fear from the fever-shaken foreigner who had mustered barely enough strength to undress and to hoist himself onto the huge four-poster bed.

From Brussels, he was on his way to Toledo, where he had been summoned to report on the state of affairs in Flanders. Up there, things went from bad to worse. He had been appointed Lieutenant Governor of Breda through the recommendation of his long-time sponsor, Padre Domingo. The monk had expected his protégé to make short shrift of any troublemakers in town, thus giving the other Spanish officials an example of thoroughness, but Vega had turned out to be the wrong man for the task.

Though ever ready to burn or behead anyone suspected of abetting the rebels, he was nonetheless afraid of weightier decisions (such as whether to hang the whole Town Council or to destroy a dike) for which the Crown would hold him accountable. Such fear had not been lost on the insurgents, who used his every weakness, every hesitation, to inch their way toward control of the place.

Gil de Vega groaned and pushed himself closer to the edge of the bed where the linen sheet was still fresh and cool. He wished he were back in Saragossa in his house on the Square San Isidro, his wife and four daughters waiting on him hand and foot.

Why had he ever gone to Flanders? Why had it taken him so long to understand that power meant little to him? He did not relish it, for it obliged him to think. He fared best when he obeyed, not when he commanded. The cardinal had seen this. Don Pedro, who could have had his choice among the scions of Spain's great families, had picked Gil de Vega as his secretary, his blind instrument. Vega had an antlike industry and was adept at furthering his own well-being beneath sharply defined duties, but he had no political vision and therefore no ambition.

He felt a vague apprehension. What was awaiting him in Spain? Where were the men of his party? What did they know? What and whom had he ignored?

His tongue was parched. He tried to grip the pitcher the servant had left on the night table, but it was out of reach. Weakly, he tugged at the bell rope, wondering whether anyone would hear him. After a while the host appeared. "Be of good cheer, sir," he said. "We have a Spanish doctor living in town. I have sent for him."

Shrove Tuesday fell late in 1587.

Vrone had the bay horse hitched to the carriage instead of the sleigh for the drive to the yearly evening dance at Town Hall.

Babeli had brought little Juan downstairs to see his parents off. They were a handsome couple, Miguel's dark, slim elegance — he was all in black except for the narrow, white-ruffled collar — no less arresting than Vrone's blond loveliness in bottle-green brocade.

Marriage and motherhood had not weighed down her fine-boned frame with any additional flesh, but the lines from her nostrils to the corners of her mouth had smoothed, and her near-sighted eyes, when not behind spectacles, squinted kindly at the world.

The child waved both of his little arms as Vrone took the reins and the carriage went off. She loved to drive, while Miguel, who preferred his mount, never used the vehicle except in her company.

The lanes thronged with disguised and masked revelers, singing, yelling, fiddling, or shaking wooden rattles. Shouts were heard. "Here they come! Here they come!"

Everybody pressed against the house walls to watch the mummers pass, men on stilts, carrying huge cardboard heads. Vrone had to halt the horse until the last monster had gone by, but when she flicked the reins again, a servant from the Twelve Apostles seized them. He had worked his way through the crowd and now breathlessly delivered his message.

Miguel sighed and Vrone snorted.

"Sick on Fastnacht! So much for Carnival. Well, climb up, Uli," she added resignedly and turned the horse around.

"I'll bet it's the beer," Vrone declared. "It does not agree with foreigners." (Miguel had become a Basler to her, although they still spoke Italian to one another.) "Just give him a laxative and an emetic, that way he'll get rid of it on both ends, and let's be off again!" Miguel laughed. When they arrived at the inn, the host was standing in the entrance; he greeted them with respect and relief.

"The gentleman is doing poorly, Doctor," he said. "I hope he won't die in my house."

While the innkeeper was accompanying her husband upstairs, Vrone entered the taproom.

A few notables — the syndic, two councillors, and the old Reverend Wyss — were having a bottle after dinner. Except for the priest, they rose from their seats.

"Why, Mistress Vrone," they welcomed her, "this is an unexpected pleasure."

She explained that her husband had been asked to see a sick Spaniard in one of the guest rooms just as she and he were driving to the Town Hall dance.

The clock struck half-past seven.

"That gives him fifteen minutes to straighten up the mischief-maker" — she laughed — "for the dance begins at eight, as you know."

"It provides us with fifteen minutes of your company, Mistress Vrone," the syndic said gallantly, moving a chair forward. She sat down with the gentlemen.

Vega was tossing and turning as the host entered, followed by Miguel.

"Sir," the man said, "here is Doctor Miguel de Roxas." He withdrew.

Miguel took one of the lighted candles from the table and walked over to the bed. The sick man was laughing hoarsely. "Miguel de Roxas — Miguel de Roxas. Can't be," he said, panting. Between groans, fits of mirth shook him. "Miguel de Roxas. You drowned. Go away."

Candle in hand, Miguel gazed at Vega's face, slowly

201

recalling the bland features he had nearly forgotten. Gil de Vega. Camacho's Don Gil. Miguel felt no blood rising to his head. His mind was as clear as ice. "Did you get it?" he asked.

"Get — what?"

"The house."

"Ye—— yes."

"You like it? Is it big enough?"

Vega's breath came in spasms. "Big enough?" he gasped. "Yes, quite big." At once, he was babbling. "I have a wife and four daughters, that's why I wanted to buy it, but the doctor wouldn't hear of it, and he alone by himself, and I have a wife and four daughters — "

Miguel cut him short. "Who told you that the Jews were in the cellar?"

"No one . . ."

"Then how? You put him on the rack?"

Vega, his eyes closed, did not answer.

Miguel grabbed him by the shoulder and jerked him up, supporting the lolling head.

"Don't die yet. You put him on the rack?"

The bloodshot eyes opened for a moment. "No need . . . He had . . . cobwebs on his shoulder . . ."

Miguel let go of Vega, who fell back on the pillows. A sudden weakness made him hold on to the bedpost while his mind, with feverish speed, retraced the path of Vega's reasoning: Juan de Roxas had entered the courtroom in his black garb, the gray-white threads clinging to his shoulder. There were no cobwebs in his study, nor anywhere near it, what with that house-proud Paca. No cobwebs save in the cellar. Why had he gone down there? To get a bottle?

Not likely. Whoever was called before the Holy Office, though only as an expert for the Crown, needed all his wits about him. So what business did he have in the cellar? Were there not three Jews missing? A swift search — Vega had sent the soldiers while Juan de Roxas was still testifying — confirmed the obvious guess. The doctor could be safely arrested.

Downstairs, Vrone looked at her watch. Quarter to eight. She excused herself from her respectful squires, left the taproom, and mounted the stairs. Candlelight was shimmering from under the door of the guest chamber. She sat down on one of the low trunks that stood along the corridor wall and waited. After a while she rose and listened, but the heavy oak panels muffled the sounds from within. She opened the door a crack.

The room was sparsely lighted by a few tapers. There was a canopied bed and a man in it, his dry tongue hanging white and swollen out of his mouth. What was this? Where was Miguel? Why had he not called for water?

But then she saw her husband. He stood near the bedpost, at one with the shadow in his black doublet, his hands clasped behind his back, staring down at the man in the bed.

He said something in Spanish, with an odd, glassy sound to his voice. Unable to make out the words, she strained her ears.

". . . a wife and four daughters," she heard now, "and no house . . ."

Guessing it all, Vrone drew in her breath and bit her fist to stifle a scream, but managed to collect herself at once. She remained standing by the door, her eyes riveted on Miguel.

He kept looking at Vega. This was the man, he knew, who had set the death trap for his father. Yet Vega had had no quarrel with the doctor. Why, then, why? For the house.

He shut his eyes for an instant as scenes of a vile domesticity passed before them: Vega taking the air in the flowered patio; Vega drinking Juan de Roxas' wine; Vega's wife and daughters trying to squeeze into Marguerite's dresses. His mind dwelled on the image of his father's study: Vega sitting in the Florentine armchair . . .

The sick man moaned. His eyes turned toward the pitcher. Miguel saw it. Was he supposed to give Vega to drink, then, he, Juan de Roxas' son? The wretch seemed to expect nothing less. A mad desire came over him to torture the man. He seized the pitcher and threw it on the ground. The water spilled and beaded over the freshly waxed floorboards. A feeble groan of terror broke from Vega's throat.

Miguel listened, bewildered. What happened? Why wasn't he gloating over the man's torment? Wasn't he avenging his father? But Juan de Roxas, he suddenly knew, would have been unimpressed by this savagery. A few rattlings and twitchings for his father's unlived years? A shabby bargain. Whoever said that revenge was sweet? It tasted like brackwater.

Vega, except for the rattling in his throat, made no other sound. Miguel, looking at him, had to make an effort to maintain a connection between his father's death and this sorry heap of bones not worth tormenting.

The pewter tankard had rolled against the bedpost. Miguel picked it up. There was still an inch of water in it, enough to fill a third of the goblet on the table.

He brought it to Vega's mouth. The drops barely relieved the cracked lips, which moved a little. "Cross," they mumbled.

"Get a priest, Veronica," Miguel said over his shoulder.

"It's that Gil de Vega, isn't it?"

"Yes. Get a priest."

She stiffened. "Not I."

He spun around and bounded to the door. Vrone held it shut, defending it with all her strength.

By God, she thought, this scoundrel dares pretend to end like a Christian! She sensed Vega's terror, his need to have his fears soothed by the censer and the oil. But let this bastard fend for himself! Miguel had given him water to drink; that was more than enough mercy!

Silently she struggled with her husband. The gasps they heard from the bed were spaced farther and farther apart, and as Miguel at last pried the door open, they ceased.

It was all over for Gil de Vega.

Exhausted, her arms hanging down, Vrone leaned against the doorjamb.

Their eyes met: hers with a look of deep satisfaction in them, his dark with weariness. He took her by the hand and led her into the hall, where he made her sit down again on the trunk. Then he went back into the room.

Amazed, he looked at the corpse. It seemed to grow more and more alien to him.

Physician again, he examined the body, still hot with fever. As he lifted the sheet he saw the man's chest and belly covered with red pustules. Of whatever illness Vega had died, he was carrying smallpox.

At once, Miguel had the corpse removed and buried in quicklime. All the secular and spiritual authorities were informed; the dance discontinued. Vega's party was sequestered, and the dead man's belongings were burned.

Those measures took several hours. Dr. Veggli, officially still town physician, had appeared at the Twelve Apostles merely to give his young Spanish colleague authority to proceed entirely according to his judgment, and had withdrawn.

Finally, at dawn, Miguel and Vrone drove home while the night watchmen warned of the danger as they called out the hours.

They went straight to the washhouse to bathe. Miguel knelt down and rekindled the fire under the huge, suspended kettle always filled with water. They sat and watched the burning logs.

"You gave him to drink," Vrone said after a while.

"I had to."

"I know. Your Hippocratic Oath."

"Certainly, but that was only part of it. The truth is, I was ashamed."

"Ashamed?"

"Yes. When I threw the pitcher on the ground, his face turned dreadful to look at. There was such fear in it — such *fawning* fear — that I felt as if I had surprised him naked. I saw him sending them to the stake and to the gallows by the hundreds . . . This grimace of cowardice was only the other side of the coin. I could not bear the sight . . ."

Vrone nodded. "I couldn't make out his face," she said, "but I, too, felt that he was mad with fear. Yet I wanted to frighten him even more . . . I should have called the priest, for your sake. Forgive me."

"Who am I to forgive you? I spilled water before a man dying of thirst . . . I, a physician. Anyway, it would have been too late."

"No," she said bravely, "there would have been time. The Reverend Wyss was in the taproom."

Miguel took her hands in his. Her truthfulness touched his heart. In an odd way, it laid to rest the ghost of the wretched man.

The water was ready. Miguel filled the wooden trough. They took off their clothes, and one by one Miguel threw them into the fire, beginning with his velvet doublet and Vrone's ball dress.

They did not go to bed after their bath. Babeli — Vrone had knocked at her window on the way to the washhouse — had brought fresh things. They dressed. After a hasty breakfast Miguel rode to Town Hall, and Vrone brought little Juan to Grellingen, a small town ten miles to the south, where Bartholomaeus' sister was living. There, the child, with Babeli in attendance, would be reasonably safe in case the disease spread in Basel.

Justina Faber, a crusty old maid, received them graciously, but installed Babeli and her ward in a back room of the house. Children, she said, should never be heard, and seen only when dry and clean, thus rarely. But when Vrone, ready to leave, turned to the carriage, little Juan began to scream. Justina took him up into her arms, soothing him.

"Drive on, Vrone!" she called over the head of the howling child. "The boy will be fine! Drive on! Your place is with your husband!"

When she arrived home, Miguel was still gone. The next weeks, she knew, would be a lonesome time.

As the days passed, Vrone went about her tasks as she had always done. She was not afraid of the pox, having passed through it at the age of three, miraculously with no more damage than a few scars on her shoulder. Everybody knew that the disease never struck twice. She had dismissed her printers and apprentices because of the quarantine, and worked alone in the shop.

Miguel, together with the other physicians in town, toiled from morning until night to prevent an epidemic; yet the isolated cases were multiplying. Vega had not been the only one to bring the disease from Flanders.

Vrone hardly saw her husband during the day. At mealtimes his seat remained empty, and at night he would fall into a sleep of exhaustion as soon as his head touched the pillow, only to be up again at dawn.

In the washhouse the fire was always burning under the water kettle, and two scullery girls could hardly keep up with the soap-making, for he would insist on taking a bath after each round and would distribute the leftover soapcakes to his patients. A thick stripe of lime chalk was poured before the threshold of every door in the house leading outside.

One afternoon Vrone was sitting at her proof-covered work table when Miguel came in and, spent, sank onto a chair.

"How does it go, Miguel?"

He frowned. "Not too good. Trudi Brechbühler died this morning."

Vrone burst into tears. Trudi, that kind, friendly woman! Why could not her good-for-nothing husband have caught the pox? And why, why this senseless suffering in the whole town?

A question rose in her mind, hard and clear. She knew she should be frightened by it, yet she felt nothing but an intense, sober wish to know. She looked over her shoulder — there was no one. "Miguel," she asked in a low voice, "do you truly believe in God? In Him without Whose will no sparrow falls from the roof?"

He put his elbow on the table, his chin into his hand, and looked her straight in the eyes. "I don't know. There are too many dead sparrows lying around."

She nodded, oddly satisfied.

"I had a colleague in Padua," he went on, again in a low voice, "who was convinced that God, the Supreme Artisan, had a workshop full of never-carried-out projects, raw sketches, broken clay models, half-finished canvases . . . and that, like every painter or sculptor, He would throw away things He had made whenever they looked crooked to Him . . . and that this was corroborated by the story of the Flood, where it says, *and God regretted that He had made Man.* Perhaps the fellow was right. God is so absorbed in His creation — He keeps on creating — that He is somewhat absent-minded from time to time. I don't think that He watches over us, watches us all the time, but He *expects* us to behave as if He watched . . ."

"That means we have to look out for ourselves . . . Miguel . . . I am scared. Let's leave town for a while. Let's pass by Grellingen, take the child, and go to the vineyard until this is over. You've done your part. Let old Veggli move a finger for a change."

He shook his head. "I cannot, Veronica. Someone must see to it that the sick get proper care, that they are isolated, that their stuff is washed, their bedstraw burned, that there is enough chalk . . . Someone must scatter the prayer meetings — crowds invite contagion, but they don't understand that. Someone must chase away the old women with their miracle cures of cow dung . . . I cannot leave those people now. They trust me. God wants one to stand in for Him as well as one can, whenever He happens to be — absentminded. So that nobody must feel, well, Godforsaken."

"Who has made you so certain of that?"

"Who? My father did. He did the right thing in the absence of God. He could have recanted. It would not have added to the plight of those poor wretches who were condemned in advance. The judge even gave him an hour to change his mind. My father refused for no *earthly* reason. I never thought it through until now."

Miguel remained seated, too weary to move. He idly took up one of the proof sheets covering the table. "A Vita of Luther . . . ?"

"Well, yes, it's for the Synod's pamphlet . . . The Frobens asked me last week to help them out. I charged them a rush fee."

He laughed. She was incorrigible. Then he looked again at the sheet and read:

. . . and it so happened that Master Michael Stifl, the widely celebrated mathematician, had calculated that the end of the world would come in the Year of Grace 1525. There was much wailing and weeping, but Dr. Luther kept a cheerful countenance. One day a friend visited Luther in

the latter's garden and found him planting an apple tree.
The friend was astonished and asked: "Why do you plant
a tree when the world is coming to end?" to which Luther
replied: "And if I knew that the world would come to an
end tomorrow, I still would plant my apple tree today."
Miguel laughed again. "Luther, what do you know!
Luther, of all people! Did he believe this prophecy? Possibly, he was pretty superstitious. But if he did, then he
planted his tree in the teeth of all his talk of predestination
and of the Unfree Will!"

Vrone had taken off her spectacles, a habit she had when
she was listening keenly. "But if this is true" — she spoke
slowly — "then he must have counted on the righteous
ones *perhaps* to turn the tide around! Then everybody has
a voice and a chance. Then maybe God does count on us
after all!"

"He may as well." St. Catherine's bell struck four. It was
time to go on yet another round. He rose. She went to him
and he took her in his arms.

"Veronica, tomorrow we will plant *our* apple tree," he
said.

Miguel dug the hole. He and Vrone knelt in the young
grass. While she held back the loose dirt, he cautiously
lowered the sapling with the dangling roots into the ground.
They smoothed the earth around it. Vrone had her copper
sprinkler ready and watered the little tree.

They rose to their feet. The air seemed light around
them. Miguel de Roxas looked at his young wife. Fear and
care had left dark circles under her eyes, yet she had never
seemed lovelier to him than on that spring morning.

He lifted his hands to take her face between them, but

as he was about to touch her, he let them sink again. He had seen a red spot on his left wrist, no larger than a pinhead. Backing off, he held up his hand and she, too, saw it. She felt faint. Within a day, she knew, Miguel would lie in a raging fever. He would die. But — would he? Perhaps not. Perhaps he would live. An angry strength filled her to her very fingertips. Perhaps she could see him through this. Did he not always say that the patient's will to live was half the battle? And Miguel would give Death no easy time; that much she knew.

The sun came through the trees covered with their small buds. Vrone looked at the beloved face bathed in light, at its beauty, which the disease would destroy even if he survived. She would remember its every feature, would keep its image in her heart through death or devastation, to describe it to her son someday — to her son, Juan de Roxas.